"I've been expecting you."

"You have?" Ellie frowned; how could he possibly have been expecting her when until half an hour ago she hadn't expected to be here herself?

"I still have Friday evening free, if you're interested. Are you interested? Ellie...?"

"I'm interested...you'll go to the Delacorte dinner with me?"

He gave a sudden grin, looking years younger, the gray eyes warm. "I thought you would never ask!"

She wouldn't have done ordinarily, and they both knew it. But nothing about this situation was ordinary.

To the rescue...armed with a ring!

Marriage is their mission!

Look for more titles in this ongoing and adventurous new series.

Available only from Harlequin Presents®.

Carole Mortimer

THE YULETIDE ENGAGEMENT

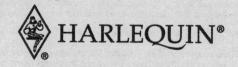

TORONTO • NEW YORK • LONDON
AMSTERDAM • PARIS • SYDNEY • HAMBURG
STOCKHOLM • ATHENS • TOKYO • MILAN • MADRID
PRAGUE • WARSAW • BUDAPEST • AUCKLAND

For
Peter

ISBN: 0-373-12364-7

THE YULETIDE ENGAGEMENT

First North American Publication 2003.

This edition published by arrangement with Harlequin Books S.A.

® and TM are trademarks of the publisher. Trademarks indicated with
® are registered in the United States Patent and Trademark Office, the
Canadian Trade Marks Office and in other countries.

Visit us at www.eHarlequin.com

Printed in U.S.A.

CHAPTER ONE

'CINDERS shall go to the ball!' Toby announced as he stood poised in the kitchen doorway, a look of triumph on his boyishly handsome face. 'Although the first person to call me the Fairy Godmother is going to get slapped!'

Ellie looked up from the newspaper she had been reading where she sat at the kitchen table, blue gaze narrowing as she took in the pleased flush on her brother's cheeks. 'Toby, did you call into the pub again on your way home from work?' she prompted suspiciously. His eyes looked overbright, and he wasn't making much sense, either!

'That's all the thanks I get for getting you out of a difficult situation—accusations of inebriation!' He grinned widely as he came fully into the kitchen, leaving the door open behind him, despite the fact that snow was forecast for later this evening.

Ellie gave an involuntary shiver as a cold blast of air followed her brother into the room. 'At least shut the door, Toby,' she reasoned with indulgent affection. 'You—'

'Didn't you hear me, Ellie?' He pulled her easily to her feet, swinging her round in the close confines of the kitchen.

'Something about Cinders and a ball.' She nodded, starting to feel slightly dizzy as the kitchen became a

5

giddy blur; maybe intoxication was infectious? 'Toby, will you please stop?' she gasped weakly.

He did, holding onto her hands as she swayed slightly. 'Ellie, I asked him and he said yes. Can you believe that?' he exclaimed happily. 'Didn't I tell you he's one of the good guys? He's even coming round later this evening to sort out the details,' he announced triumphantly. 'Isn't that just—?'

'Toby, will you just slow down and tell me who you have asked to do what?' Ellie cut in impatiently, but she already felt a terrible sense of foreboding as it slowly started to dawn on her exactly what Toby might have done. Surely he hadn't—he wouldn't have—? She had been joking, for goodness' sake!

Toby let go of her hands, grinning at her victoriously as he reached for an apple from the bowl in the middle of the kitchen table, biting down on its crispness with complete enjoyment.

'Toby!' Ellie said warningly. 'Will you just tell me exactly what it is you've done?' Although she had a feeling she already knew the answer to that!

Her brother returned her gaze with guileless blue eyes. 'I've asked Patrick to escort you to your company Christmas dinner, of course,' he dismissed with satisfaction.

'Patrick...?' she echoed faintly.

'Patrick McGrath. My boss,' her brother enlarged impatiently as she just stared at him. 'Remember? We were discussing the problem at the weekend and you said that what you really needed was someone high-powered like Patrick to accompany you. That way—'

'But I wasn't being serious, Toby,' she cut in incredulously, sinking back down onto the kitchen chair, staring disbelievingly at her brother. He was the younger by only a year, but sometimes—like now—it could feel like ten!

The company Christmas dinner was quickly looming, and this year, after Ellie's recent break-up with Gareth, a junior partner in the law firm they both worked for, it promised to be something of an ordeal for her. Not to go would give the impression she was too much of a coward to face Gareth and his new girlfriend, but to go on her own would make it look as if she were still pining for him. Which she most certainly was not!

Which was why, over the weekend, as she and Toby had lingered over their meal together on Sunday evening, she had drunk one glass of wine too many and suggested that she needed someone like Patrick McGrath, Toby's wealthy entrepreneurial boss, to go with her to the dinner—no one could possibly think she was still interested in Gareth when she was in the company of such a man.

Tall, dark, handsome and extremely successful, Patrick McGrath was the ideal man to allay any doubts anyone might have as to her having any lingering feelings for Gareth.

But she had thought Toby knew that it had only been that third glass of wine talking, that she hadn't really meant for it to happen!

She closed her eyes now in pained disbelief. 'Toby, please, please tell me you haven't really asked Patrick McGrath to take me out next week,' she groaned desperately.

Her brother paused in the act of taking another bite

of his apple. 'I haven't?' he said uncertainly, some of the look of triumph starting to fade from his face as he finally noticed Ellie's marked lack of enthusiasm.

'You haven't!' she repeated firmly.

She had met Toby's boss only once, five months ago. It had been enough. There was no doubting that Patrick McGrath was very rich, very self-assured, and very eligible. In fact, the very last person Ellie would ever want to ask her out!

Toby looked puzzled. 'But on Sunday night you said—'

'I had drunk too much wine, for goodness' sake,' Ellie stood up to pace the confines of the room. 'I wasn't being serious—I just thought of the most unlikely person ever to—I didn't really *mean* it when I said—'

'Patrick would make the perfect escort for your dinner a week on Friday,' Toby finished obligingly.

She winced as she remembered saying exactly that. But it was a situation that required an extreme solution for unusual circumstances. On Sunday evening she had run the gamut of them, and had suggested Patrick McGrath being the perfect escort as the most extreme of those extremes. She certainly hadn't expected Toby to act on it!

'Exactly,' she confirmed weakly. 'Toby, please tell me you didn't—'

'But I did,' Toby told her impatiently. 'I asked Patrick to accompany you. And as he said yes I can't see what your problem is.' He shook his head.

He couldn't see—! The problem was that Ellie felt

totally ridiculous and completely humiliated. She had no intention of—of—

'Toby, you can just call the man right now and tell him not to come here this evening—that you made a mistake, that your sister doesn't need an escort next Friday or any other time, and that if or when I do need an escort I'll find one of my own, thank you very much!' She glared her indignation at her irresponsible brother.

Blue eyes blazed at the thought of her humiliation if she should ever meet Patrick McGrath again. Her dark, shoulder-length hair seemed to crackle with the force of her anger, every inch of her five-foot-two-inch frame seeming to bristle with indignation.

'But—'

'Call him, Toby,' she repeated with cold fury. 'Call Patrick McGrath right now and tell him!'

'But—'

'Now, Toby!' she ground out forcefully.

'I think what your brother is trying to tell you—Ellie, isn't it?—is that there's no need for him to call and tell me anything—I'm already standing right here,' drawled a lazily amused voice from directly behind her.

Ellie had spun round at the first sound of that drawling voice, having to arch her neck back in order to look up into the confident face of Patrick McGrath.

If ever she had wanted the ground to open and swallow her up it was right now.

Patrick McGrath!

Tall—well over six feet. Dark—hair kept deliberately short as it looked inclined to curl. Handsome—grey eyes beneath arched dark brows, an arrogant slash of a nose, chiselled lips that were curved into a smile at the moment, an out-of-season tan darkening those distinctive features. Successful—even the casual clothes he was wearing this evening—a black silk shirt and faded denims—obviously bore a designer label, and the black leather shoes were no doubt hand-made.

'So, Ellie,' he drawled softly. 'What was it you wanted Toby to tell me?'

She was trying to speak, really she was; she just couldn't seem to get any words to come out of her throat!

'The details for next Friday, perhaps?' Patrick McGrath prompted interestedly, grey gaze lightly mocking.

How Ellie remembered that mocking gaze. How could she ever forget it? Toby still had no idea what had actually happened at her one and only other meeting with this man; Ellie hadn't told him, and as the days and weeks had passed, without Toby making any reference to it, it had eventually become obvious that Patrick McGrath wasn't going to tell her brother all the details of that meeting, either.

But Ellie was unlikely to ever forget them!

It had been an unusually hot summer this year, with everyone wearing the minimum of clothing, and Ellie, conscious of her impending summer holiday abroad and with a wish not to stand out like a sore thumb on the Majorcan beaches, had decided to spend one Saturday afternoon sunbathing in their secluded back garden.

Topless.

How could she have known that Patrick McGrath had been telephoning for over an hour, urgently trying to contact Toby? That he had decided to come over to the house in person when he'd received no reply? Or that he would stroll out into the garden when he found the house unlocked but seemingly deserted?

Ellie had made a mad scramble for her top when she'd realised she was no longer alone, but it hadn't been quick enough to prevent that piercing gaze from having a full view of her naked breasts.

Damn it, she was sure she could see the knowledge of that memory now, clearly gleaming in those mocking grey eyes.

Despite what she might have said on Sunday evening, warmed by the unaccustomed wine, Patrick McGrath was the last man she wanted to accompany her anywhere!

She drew in a deep breath. 'Toby has— He was mistaken when he asked—I'm sorry you've been troubled, Mr McGrath.' She spoke dismissively, her gaze fixed on the second button of his black silk shirt. 'I never meant—'

'Toby, why don't you make us all some coffee?' Patrick McGrath turned to the younger man authoritatively. 'While Ellie and I sort out whether or not I'm being stood up a week on Friday,' he added derisively.

Toby set about making the pot of coffee and Ellie looked up at Patrick McGrath reprovingly. He might find all this funny, but she certainly didn't. As if any woman would ever stand this man up!

But they did need to sort this mess out, and she would rather do it out of earshot of her well-meaning but unthinking younger brother.

'Let's go through to the sitting room, Mr McGrath,'

she suggested briskly, some of her normal self confidence returning as she led the way down the hallway to their lounge.

She was twenty-seven years old, had cared for Toby since their parents were killed in a car crash eight years ago, taking over the running of the family home as well as continuing her full-time job as secretary, eventually to one of the senior partners in a prestigious law firm. She was more than up to dealing with this situation.

Well...ordinarily she could be up to dealing with it, she conceded as Patrick McGrath stood in the middle of the sitting-room, looking at her with his laughing steely eyes.

How on earth did Toby cope with working for this man every day? she wondered frowningly. He had such presence, such confidence, that just being in the same room with him was a little overpowering. But she knew Toby thought the other man was wonderful, that her brother thoroughly enjoyed his job as this man's personal assistant.

Maybe it was only women who found Patrick McGrath overpowering...?

Well...one woman, Ellie conceded self-derisively. Maybe if she weren't so completely aware of the fact that this man had seen her sunbathing topless—

Stop that right now, Ellie, she told herself firmly. If she was going to sort this situation out at all then she had to put that embarrassing memory completely from her mind. Although it would help if Patrick McGrath were to do the same...

His next words didn't seem to imply that was the case!

'I don't believe the two of us have ever been formally

introduced,' he drawled softly, with an emphasis on the
'formally', it seemed to a slightly flustered Ellie. How
could she possibly have formally introduced herself
while at the same time clutching a top in front of her
naked breasts?

'Probably not,' she conceded abruptly. 'But I'm sure
you're aware that I'm Ellie Fairfax, Toby's older sister,
and I am aware you're Patrick T. McGrath—Toby's
boss.'

He gave an acknowledging inclination of his head.
'The T stands for Timothy, by the way. And Ellie is
short for...?'

'Elizabeth,' she supplied dismissively. 'Although
what—?'

'It may come up in conversation a week on Friday.'
He shrugged broad shoulders.

'Mr McGrath, there isn't going to be any "a week
on Friday".' She sighed frustratedly. 'I have no idea
what my irresponsible brother may have told you,
but—'

'He adores you, you know,' Patrick McGrath cut in
softly.

She felt the warmth in her cheeks at this completely
unexpected comment. 'I love him too.' She nodded.
'Although I don't really think that's relevant to our conversation.' She frowned.

'Ellie, do you think we could both sit down?' Patrick
McGrath suggested gently. 'At the moment we look
like two opponents about to face each other in the ring,'
he added dryly.

Maybe because that was exactly how he made her
feel—totally on the defensive! 'Please—do sit down,'
she invited abruptly.

'After you,' he drawled politely.

Ellie looked at him impatiently, finding herself the focus of Patrick McGrath's cool grey gaze as he waited for her to be seated before he would sit down himself.

Old-fashioned good manners, as well as all those other attributes!

Ellie sat down abruptly, determinedly putting those 'other attributes' firmly from her mind. 'I accept that Toby meant well when he—when he spoke to you today—' she began huskily, stopping to look enquiringly at Patrick McGrath when he began to smile.

'Sorry.' He continued to smile. 'Toby is—he's one of the least selfish people I've ever met. As well as being completely honest, utterly trustworthy and totally candid.' He sobered slightly. 'You've done a lot for him, Ellie,' he told her admiringly.

The warmth deepened in her cheeks at this even more unexpected compliment. 'I'm pleased he's working out so well as your assistant.'

'I wasn't just talking about him as my assistant, Ellie,' Patrick McGrath cut in impatiently. 'Toby is an exceptional young man. And it's all thanks to you,' he added firmly.

She gave a rueful smile. 'I think my parents may have had something to do with it.'

'Your parents were killed when Toby was eighteen.' He shook his head. 'A very dangerous time for a young man to be left without guidance.'

Ellie frowned. 'You were right about Toby being candid!' It made her wonder exactly what else Toby had confided to Patrick McGrath about their private family affairs.

He looked at her quizzically. 'You should be proud of him, Ellie, not—'

'Here we are.' Toby was grinning widely as he kicked the door open with his foot and came in with the tray of coffee things.

Ellie looked up at him affectionately; she *was* proud of him—of the way he had carried on with his plans to go to university to study law after the accident that had killed their parents, of the way he had obtained a first-class degree, of the way he had worked doggedly in a law firm for the two years following, before applying and succeeding in getting this position with Patrick McGrath. Yes, she was very proud of him—she just wished that she had taught him to be a little less candid when it came to their own private affairs!

'All settled?' He sat back on his heels to look at them both expectantly after placing the tray down on the low table.

'Almost.' Patrick McGrath was the one to answer him dryly.

Almost nothing! Ellie was grateful to him for his praise of Toby and of the part she had played in helping to form him into the likeable young man he was—but that did not mean she was going to agree to this ridiculous plan for Patrick McGrath to accompany her to the company Christmas dinner!

'We just have to dot the ''i''s and cross the ''t''s,' Patrick McGrath assured the younger man.

'Really?' Toby looked pleased by the prospect as he stood up. 'I have a date later, so if neither of you mind I'll just go upstairs and change while you two chat. Be

back in a couple of minutes,' he added, before leaving
the room.

'You see what I mean,' Patrick McGrath murmured
softly. 'He's like a puppy, or a little brother that you
don't want to disappoint.'

'He happens to *be* a little brother,' Ellie reminded
him frustratedly. 'And I'm afraid this time he's going
to be very disappointed!'

'Why?' Patrick McGrath regarded her with cool eyes.

'Because—because, Mr McGrath—' she began impatiently.

'Patrick,' he invited smoothly.

'Very well—Patrick,' she bit out decisively.

'Has something changed since Toby spoke to me this
afternoon?' he prompted interestedly. 'Have you and
the ex-boyfriend managed to patch things up after all?
Because if you have—'

'No, we haven't managed to "patch things up",' she
cut in evenly, her frustration increasing by the minute
as she felt this situation slipping more and more out of
her grasp. 'And we never will,' she added firmly. 'But
that does not mean—'

'You have to go to the dinner with me instead,'
Patrick McGrath finished slowly. 'Do you have someone else in mind?'

'No. But—'

'Then where's your problem? I was asked; I said
yes—'

'You're starting to sound like Toby now,' she interrupted weakly. 'Mr—Patrick,' she corrected as he
raised his brows in silent rebuke, 'you can't seriously

want to come to a boring company dinner as my escort!'

'Why can't I?'

'Because it will be *boring*!' she assured him heatedly. What was wrong with the man? Couldn't he see she didn't want him to go with her?

His mouth twisted into the semblance of a smile. 'Ellie, I think you underestimate yourself,' he drawled huskily.

'I wasn't—' She broke off, her cheeks fiery red. 'Look, Patrick, Toby shouldn't have told you any of those things about my personal life. Because they are personal. And, quite frankly—'

'A little embarassing?' he finished calmly, obviously having taken note of her red cheeks.

A little? This had to be the worst thing Toby had ever done to her. Honest and trustworthy were fine, candid she really needed to discuss with him!

'Yes, it's embarrassing.' Ellie sighed heavily. 'And, apart from the fact that you value Toby as your employee, I have no idea why you should even have listened to his suggestion, let alone actually contemplated going through with it.' She was totally exasperated with both men, and she didn't mind Patrick McGrath knowing it.

His eyes met her gaze unwaveringly for long seconds. 'Can't you?' he finally murmured softly.

Ellie frowned at him. Was that a smile she saw lurking on the edges of those sculptured lips? And was that a faint knowing gleam she detected in the depths of those grey eyes?

She had an instant flashback to that scene in the gar-

den five months ago, of her panicked grab for her top
when she realized she was no longer alone, her eyes
wide with dismay as she stared across the garden at the
stranger standing there watching her with amused grey
eyes.

The same amused grey eyes that were looking across
the sitting room at her right now!

'Besides, Ellie,' Patrick drawled huskily, 'why
should you be the one to feel embarrassed because
some man was too much of an idiot to appreciate what
he had?'

There was a compliment in there somewhere—if she
could only find it.

'That's isn't the reason I feel embarrassed,' she assured him dismissively. 'My broken relationship is—
was private. I just can't believe Toby has been so indiscreet as to ask you to be my dinner partner next
week.' She shook her head disgustedly.

'You were going to ask me yourself?'

'Of course not,' she answered impatiently.

What was wrong with these two men? Couldn't they
see that it was humiliating that either of them had
thought she was incapable of finding a dinner partner
for herself?

'Well, as I had no idea of the dinner until Toby told
me about it, I could hardly have been the one to do the
asking,' Patrick reasoned lightly.

As if he would have asked her anyway; it was obvious he had only agreed to the suggestion now for
Toby's sake.

'Look, Toby meant well,' Patrick insisted when he

could see she was about to protest once again. 'He's— just concerned for your happiness,' he added evenly.

'But he has no reason to be,' she protested. 'I'm twenty-seven, not twelve.'

His mouth quirked into a teasing smile. 'I don't think anyone is disputing your maturity, Ellie,' he murmured tauntingly.

So he did remember that afternoon in the garden as well as she did!

'If anything,' he continued frowningly, 'it's the opposite, I think.'

Now it was Ellie's turn to frown. 'What do you mean?'

'Nothing,' he dismissed abruptly, standing up. 'And if you're absolutely sure about not needing an escort next Friday…?'

'I'm sure,' she said firmly.

Much as she would have enjoyed sweeping into the restaurant on the arm of this attractive and successful man, if only to see the stunned look on Gareth's face, she knew that she really couldn't do it under these circumstances.

'It isn't that I'm not grateful.' She grimaced.

'Just thanks but no thanks?' Patrick mused.

'Yes,' she sighed.

He nodded. 'Then I'm obviously wasting our time,' he added briskly. 'I trust you'll explain the situation to Toby when he comes down? Tell him that at least I tried, hmm?'

'The coffee…' she reminded him lamely, belatedly

realizing she had made no effort to offer to pour him a cup.

He smiled humourlessly. 'We both know that was just a ploy to keep Toby busy while the two of us talked.'

'Yes.' Ellie sighed again, moving to accompany him from the room.

Patrick paused in the open doorway. 'Don't be too hard on Toby, hmm?' he encouraged softly. 'He feels a certain—responsibility where your happiness is concerned.'

'I'll try to bear that in mind,' she assured him dryly.

'Ellie...?'

She looked up, her breath catching in her throat as she found herself the focus of Patrick's McGrath's enigmatic grey gaze.

He really was the most gorgeous-looking man, she acknowledged weakly. All six foot two inches of him!

'You know where I am if you should change your mind...' he told her pointedly.

Yes, he was gorgeous, and there was no doubt that having him as her escort would have salvaged her damaged pride—just as there was no doubt she had no intention of taking him up on his offer!

'I won't,' she assured him with finality.

How could Ellie have known, how could she possibly have guessed, that something disastrous would occur during the following week—something that would necessitate her not only changing her mind, but having to go to Patrick McGrath herself and ask him if he would consider coming to the company dinner with her after all?

CHAPTER TWO

'How do I look?' She grimaced at Toby questioningly as she entered the kitchen where her brother sat eating the dinner she had prepared for him before getting ready for her evening out.

'You look great,' he assured her enthusiastically. 'New dress?' he observed teasingly.

Of course it was a new dress; she couldn't go out with Patrick McGrath wearing the old trusty little-black-dress that she had worn to last year's company Christmas dinner. No, as Patrick's dinner date she wanted to wear something much more stylish. And noticeable.

She had known as soon as she saw the knee-length figure-hugging red dress in the shop that it would ensure, once and for all, that Gareth was no longer under any misapprehension concerning her having fully got over him. Especially with Patrick McGrath as her dinner partner!

'Do you like it?' she asked her brother uncertainly.

Trying the dress on in the shop and actually putting it on at home were two different things, she had realised a few minutes ago. Seen in this homely setting, the dress was much more revealing than anything Ellie had ever worn before, clinging to her slenderness in a bright red swathe, the low neckline and sleeveless style showing arms and throat still lightly tanned from her holiday in the summer.

Her hair was swept up loosely from the slenderness of her neck and secured with two gold combs. The change in hairstyle seemed to enlarge her eyes and the dark sweep of her lashes. Blusher highlighted her cheeks, and the bright red gloss on her lips was the same colour as the dress.

Ellie had noted all of this in her bedroom mirror a few minutes ago, sweeping out of the room and down the stairs before she had time for second thoughts and settled for the familiar black dress after all.

'You look wonderful, sis,' Toby told her, sitting back to look at her admiringly. 'You're going to knock him off his feet!'

She frowned. 'Toby, the idea isn't for me to attract Patrick McGrath—'

'I was referring to Gareth,' he murmured pointedly.

'Oh…Gareth,' she acknowledged weakly, feeling the colour warming her cheeks at her mistake. In all honesty she had totally forgotten about Gareth as she prepared for her evening out. Which was ridiculous when he was the reason she had gone to all this trouble in the first place.

The reason she had swallowed her pride and gone to Patrick, and told him she had changed her mind after all!

To give the man his due, he hadn't batted an eyelid when she had turned up at his office three days ago—without an appointment—and asked him if he was still agreeable to going out with her on Friday evening.

She had acted instinctively, knowing that if she gave

herself time to think about whether or not she should go and see him she would change her mind. Although she had been a little thrown by his opening comment!

'I've been expecting you.' He put his gold pen down on top of the papers on his desk before smiling across at her as she stood just inside his office, his secretary having closed the door behind her as she left.

'You have?' Ellie frowned; how could he possibly have been expecting her when until half an hour ago she hadn't expected to be here herself?

'Call it a hunch.' He nodded. 'You can sit down, you know, Ellie,' he added mockingly. 'There's no charge!'

He seemed different today, Ellie realized, more the thirty-eight-year-old successful businessman that he was. He was dressed formally too, in a dark grey suit with a white silk shirt, a light grey tie knotted meticulously at his throat.

She made no move to sit in the chair he indicated, knowing that she had made a mistake in coming here today, that she should have taken the time to think after all, that—

'I still have Friday evening free, if you're interested,' he told her huskily.

Her eyes widened. 'You do?'

He nodded. 'Are you interested?'

She swallowed hard, wishing she could say no but knowing that, after what she had learnt today, she badly needed this man's presence at her side on Friday evening—for moral support if nothing else.

'Ellie...?' he prompted at her continued silence.

'I'm interested,' she admitted abruptly.

'Has something happened?' he asked shrewdly.

Had something happened! Gareth, that selfish, un-thinking, uncaring—

'Something's happened,' Patrick acknowledged rue-fully, standing up to pour her a cup of coffee from the hot percolator that stood on the side. 'I'm sorry it's nothing stronger,' he apologised dryly as he handed her the cup and saucer. 'You look as if you could do with a double whisky!'

'I don't drink whisky,' she said vaguely, taking a sip of the hot coffee. Not because she thought it would make her feel any better, more for something to do with her shaking hands.

Cold hands, she realised belatedly as she wrapped them about the cup; the snow that had been threatening to fall all week had finally come tumbling down this morning. And in her agitation Ellie had completely for-gotten to collect her outer coat and gloves before leav-ing the office earlier.

'Is it anything I should know about?' Patrick gently urged.

'Anything…? It isn't Toby, if that's what you're worried about,' she hastened to reassure him.

'I didn't think for a moment that it was; as far as I'm aware Toby is in York today, with—with another of my employees,' Patrick dismissed lightly. 'I wish you would sit down, Ellie,' he said softly.

Of course. He wouldn't sit down if she didn't. Ellie sat, the cup rattling precariously in the saucer as she did so.

Patrick moved back to sit behind his desk. 'Take your

time,' he invited. 'I don't have any appointments for a couple of hours.'

'It isn't going to take me that long to—!' She broke off, her face pale as she brought herself under control. 'My ex-boyfriend intends announcing his engagement at the dinner on Friday evening,' she bit out reluctantly.

'Ah,' Patrick murmured comprehendingly.

Ellie looked across at him sharply. 'It doesn't bother me,' she assured him.

He raised dark brows. 'It doesn't?'

'Look, Mr—Patrick,' she amended as he raised those brows even higher. 'I don't know what Toby told you about the end of my relationship with Gareth, but—'

'Nothing at all, as it happens,' he assured her dryly. 'Toby can be discreet when he needs to be,' he added at her sceptical look. 'He wouldn't have lasted long as my assistant if he couldn't!'

'Yes. Well.' Ellie grimaced. 'I was the one to end my relationship with Gareth.'

Patrick frowned. 'Then why—?'

'He told everyone at the office that *he* was the one to end it,' Ellie recalled disgustedly. 'And when he was seen with someone else only a few days later...!' She shook her head. 'If I had tried to contradict his story then I would have just looked like "a woman scorned",' she reasoned heavily.

'Hmm. Just out of interest—why *did* you stop seeing him?' Patrick asked interestedly.

'Because—' She drew in a deep breath, shaking her head. 'I think that also comes under the heading of "Private",' she told him stiffly.

'Okay,' he conceded reluctantly. 'But if you aren't bothered by his engagement…?'

'I'm really not,' she insisted firmly. 'At least, only so far as… I have to work with all these people, Patrick.' She grimaced. 'Gareth informed me a couple of hours ago about the engagement announcement.'

'Big of him,' Patrick bit out scathingly.

It had been more out of spite, actually, but she was way past caring about anything Gareth did or said to her. 'If I turn up alone on Friday evening and the announcement is made—'

'All your work colleagues are going to end up feeling sorry for you,' Patrick acknowledged hardly.

Her eyes flashed deeply blue. 'Yes!' And the pity of people she worked with on a daily basis—even misplaced pity—was something she just couldn't bear to think about.

Even if it meant coming to this man and admitting she had made a mistake in so arbitrarily refusing his offer to act as her escort at the dinner!

'If you agree—if you're still willing—it will be a purely business arrangement if you consent to accompany me on Friday evening,' she told him coolly. 'I will, of course, be paying any expenses you may incur—including the petrol to get us there, any drinks we have to buy, the—'

'Stop right there, Ellie,' Patrick cut in firmly. 'When I take a woman out for the evening I do the paying. Okay?

'No, it is not okay,' she came back, just as determinedly. 'I'm taking you out. That means I pay. What do you mean, no?' She frowned as he shook his head.

'I'll only agree to go if I take you. Otherwise the deal is off, Ellie,' he added decisively.

'But this isn't one of your business deals—' she broke off as she realised *she* had been the one to say Friday evening was to be treated on a businesslike footing.

Patrick laughed softly. 'Ellie, isn't the important thing here to show this Gareth that you're more than capable of attracting a man other than him? Which, of course, you obviously are,' he continued, his grey gaze sweeping over her with slow appreciation.

Ellie was dressed in one of the suits she wore to work, a fitted black one today, teamed with a blue blouse. Slightly damp from the snow still falling outside!

Ellie was under no illusions as regarded her looks; at best they could be called pleasant. She was neither fat nor too thin, and her hair—her one good feature as far as she was concerned—was always kept clean and well-styled. Her eyes were a clear blue, her lashes thick and dark, her skin smooth and creamy, but other than that her features were nondescript.

Which was why, when Gareth had joined the company six months ago—a blond Adonis with warm blue eyes and a charm that drew women to him like bees around honey—Ellie had been completely bowled over by his marked interest in her.

But she had definitely learnt her lesson where that sort of flattery and attention were concerned, which was why she knew that Patrick McGrath was just being polite now.

He was watching her with narrowed eyes. 'How long is it since the two of you broke up?'

'What does that have to do with anything?' she came back stiffly.

Patrick shrugged. 'I was merely wondering why you don't already have a new boyfriend.'

She gave a humourless smile. 'Because after my experience with Gareth I have no interest at the moment in finding myself a new boyfriend!'

'This gets more and more intriguing by the minute,' Patrick murmured interestedly.

Ellie shot him a reproving look. 'Believe me, it really isn't,' she assured him dismissively.

'So it's easier to ask me, a complete stranger, to go to your company dinner with you than it is to complicate matters with a genuine new boyfriend?' Patrick murmured consideringly. 'It makes a certain sense, I suppose.' He shrugged.

Ellie frowned. 'It does?' It sounded rather cold and contrived to her, but other than not going to the dinner at all—which was impossible now that Gareth had told her of the pending announcement of his engagement; she simply wouldn't give him the satisfaction of just not turning up!—she couldn't see any other way round the problem.

'It does,' he assured her enigmatically. 'Well, as I've already said, Ellie, I still have the evening free on Friday.'

She drew in a deep breath. 'Then you'll go to the Delacorte dinner with me?'

He gave a sudden grin, looking years younger, his grey eyes warm. 'I thought you would never ask!'

She wouldn't have done ordinarily, and they both knew it. But nothing about this situation was ordinary.

*   *   *

Which was why she was standing here, wearing a revealing red dress and more make-up than she had ever worn before, feeling decidedly like the overdressed Christmas tree that adorned their sitting room—waiting for Patrick McGrath to arrive...

He was late.

It was already seven forty-five, and before Ellie had left his office three days ago they had agreed that he would pick her up at seven-thirty, in order for them to drive to the restaurant and arrive a polite ten or fifteen minutes late for pre-dinner drinks. At this rate they would be lucky to arrive in time for the serving of the first course!

'Is he always this unpunctual?' She frowned at Toby as he cleared away his dinner things, before getting ready to go out himself.

'He'll be here, sis,' Toby dismissed assuredly. 'But I have to leave now.' He glanced up at the kitchen clock. 'I told Tess I would pick her up just after eight,' he added apologetically. He was going to the cinema this evening with his girlfriend of the last two months. 'Do you want me to try reaching Patrick on his mobile before I leave? Maybe the car broke down or something.'

'Do Mercedes break down?' Ellie came back dryly, wondering if she was going to get to 'the ball', after all!

'Mine doesn't,' drawled a familiar voice.

Ellie gasped, spinning round to face Patrick as he stood in the doorway. She was glad she had already gasped—otherwise she would have done so now; he looked absolutely breathtaking in a dinner suit!

'I wish you wouldn't keep creeping up on me like that,' she complained, to cover up the confusion she felt at his appearance.

Was anyone supposed to be this handsome? This suavely sophisticated? This—this breathtaking? There really was no other word for Patrick's appearance this evening.

'Will I do?' He arched mocking brows at her as she continued to stare at him.

Would he do as what? As a more than adequate replacement for Gareth? Certainly. As a means for making every other woman in the room jealous of her good fortune in having him as her partner for the evening? Assuredly. As a calm and soothing balm to her already battered emotions? Definitely not!

He was a one-evening-only companion—just a shield for what promised to be a very difficult evening for her. He wasn't supposed to make her pulse flutter, her knees feel weak, her insides as if they were turning to jelly!

'Ellie is feeling a little—tense this evening, Patrick,' Toby excused her lightly, picking up his jacket from the back of the chair before walking over to the door. 'Have a good evening. Want me to wait up for you, Ellie?' he added mischievously, dark brows raised teasingly.

'No, thank you!' She shot him a reproving look as he ducked out of the doorway, grinning widely as he raised a hand in farewell before disappearing into the darkness.

'We aren't going to be late back this evening, are

we, Ellie?' Patrick looked down at her mockingly. 'Only I'm usually in bed by ten-thirty.'

Ellie would hazard a guess that the only reason this man would be in bed by ten-thirty at night would be because he wasn't there alone!

'You're late,' she told him sharply, more flustered that she had just had such a thought about Patrick's nocturnal habits than she actually was by his tardiness.

'Only a few minutes,' he dismissed unconcernedly. 'I stopped along the way to buy you this.'

'This' was a corsage, a single red rose, newly in bud, made even more beautiful by the melted snowflakes clinging to the dewy petals.

Ellie blinked hard before looking up at Patrick, hastily looking down again as he returned her gaze with slightly challenging eyes. Bringing her a rose, red or otherwise, was not very businesslike. And they both knew it. But then Patrick had warned her three days ago that he intended doing this his way...

'Thank you,' she accepted huskily, taking the rose and the pin he held out to her.

'Would you like me to—?'

'No! No, thank you.' She tried to refuse his offer of help less abruptly, at the same time giving him a sceptical glance. 'I can manage.' And to prove it she attached the rose to her dress at the first try.

'I thought you might,' he murmured ruefully. 'I suppose we should be on our way, then.'

'I suppose we should,' she echoed dryly, inwardly chiding herself for the fact that she was a little disappointed he hadn't mentioned her new dress, or anything else about her appearance.

Not that she had mentioned how gorgeous he looked either; it simply wasn't in keeping, she accepted, with their arrangement.

'What a pity,' Patrick murmured as he watched her pull on her long black winter coat. 'You look absolutely stunning in that dress; it's a shame to hide it beneath that coat,' he explained as Ellie looked up at him questioningly.

'Thank you.' She felt an inner glow now rather than the outer warmth of the coat.

'Hmm,' Patrick nodded as they went out to the car, opening the door for her to get in. 'Gareth can just eat his heart out,' he added with satisfaction.

'That's what Toby said!' She laughed to cover her flushed pleasure at his compliment.

'And, as we both know, Toby wouldn't tell you a lie,' he reminded her teasingly.

No, Toby wouldn't tell her a lie—at least, not a major one—but she had a feeling this man was more than capable of practising the subtle art of subterfuge if he thought the occasion warranted it. There was a steely edge to Patrick McGrath, a ruthlessness that obviously made him such a success in business.

But Ellie dismissed both Patrick's compliments and thoughts of that steely edge as they neared the restaurant where all the other Delacorte, Delacorte and Delacorte staff would already be gathered. No doubt all believing, with the lateness of the hour, that she had decided not to attend after all.

'Everything is going to be just fine, Ellie.' Patrick

reached out in the warm confines of the car and gave her restless hands a reassuring squeeze before returning his own hand to the steering wheel of his Mercedes sports car. 'Trust me, hmm?' he encouraged as she glanced at him with troubled eyes.

She wasn't sure, after Gareth's duplicity, that she would ever completely trust another man again. But Patrick wasn't asking her to trust him in that way…

'I don't believe I've ever thanked you for agreeing to help me out like this,' she murmured ruefully. Mainly because she had been too embarrassed by her need for him to be here to actually get around to thanking him!

'I believe you did mention the word gratitude once,' he drawled. 'But that was last week—when you were turning me down.'

Before she'd had to go back and tell him the situation had indeed changed!

'Ellie, why don't we wait until the end of the evening and see if you still want to thank me then, hmm?'

Ellie shot him a sharp look; that sounded a little ominous.

'Don't look so worried, Ellie.' He chuckled after a brief glance in her direction. 'I promise to be the soul of discretion this evening.'

'You do?' She eyed him doubtfully.

After all, what did she really know about this man? Only what Toby had told her. Which, now that she thought about it, really wasn't much. Maybe Toby *could* be discreet if he needed to be! At least as far as Patrick McGrath was concerned…

Thirty-eight. Extremely successful. Single—which was probably all she really needed to know. Except... For all she knew the man might be a terrible flirt, or become terribly loud after a couple of drinks. In which case having him as her escort could prove more of a liability than a plus!

'Of course, Ellie,' he answered blandly. 'I'll try very hard not to mention to anyone that you occasionally like to sunbathe topless in the back garden—weather permitting!' He grimaced as snow slowly began to fall on the windscreen.

'You—!' Ellie gasped, feeling the sudden heat in her cheeks as she turned to stare at him. 'Patrick—'

'Ah, here we are,' he informed her lightly, turning the Mercedes into the car park of the restaurant, parking it beside the green Rolls Royce owned by Ellie's boss before getting out of the car and coming round to open Ellie's door for her. 'Was it something I said?' he prompted innocently as she made no move to get out of the car.

He knew very well that it was!

'Come on, Ellie. I'm getting wet out here,' he encouraged briskly.

Of course he was; the snow was coming down in earnest now. Ellie wrapped her coat around her and pulled up the collar about her neck as they hurried over to the entrance to the restaurant.

'We'll leave this here, I think,' Patrick said firmly as they entered the foyer, removing Ellie's coat and handing it to the receptionist before Ellie even had time to realise what he was doing.

She suddenly felt self-conscious again as she looked

down at the eye-catching red dress. Maybe it was too much. After all, this was only a company Christmas dinner. Instead of looking eye-catching, as she had hoped, was she going to look ridiculously overdressed?

'Ellie, you look beautiful,' Patrick told her firmly—before his lips came down gently on hers and his arms moved about her waist to mould her body against the hardness of his.

The kiss was so unexpected that Ellie responded, her lips parting beneath his even as her arms moved up about his shoulders.

She totally forgot where they were, why they were there—who she was, even—as those warmly sensual lips continued to explore the softness of her own. The tip of Patrick's tongue was now moving erotically against her lower lip, turning her body to liquid fire, her legs to jelly.

His eyes were dark with query as he finally lifted his head to look into the flushed beauty of her face. 'Better.' He nodded, his thumb running lightly across her slightly swollen lips. 'Now you actually look like a woman out for the evening with her lover!' he added with satisfaction.

Of course. That was the reason Patrick had kissed her. The only reason.

'Perhaps next time you could give me some warning of what you're about to do,' she bit out abruptly, covering her confusion—and her blushes!—by opening her evening bag and searching through its contents. 'Lipstick,' she told him abruptly, and held out a tissue for him to wipe his mouth.

'You do it,' Patrick encouraged huskily. 'I can't see what I'm doing,' he reasoned before she protested.

She swallowed hard, willing her heart to stop pounding, her hand not to shake as she reached up to wipe the smears of lipstick that he now had on his mouth.

So engrossed was she in not betraying how shaken she felt that she didn't even see the man walking past, a dark scowl on his handsome features as he stopped to stare at the two of them.

'Ellie…?' he questioned uncertainly—as if he couldn't quite believe the woman in the red dress, a woman who had obviously just been very thoroughly kissed, was actually her.

She stiffened before looking at him. 'Gareth,' she greeted him distantly, feeling rather than seeing Patrick as he moved to stand beside her, his arm curving possessively about her waist. She glanced up at him, a shiver running down her spine as she saw the narrow-eyed look he was giving the younger man. 'Patrick, this is a work colleague—Gareth Davies,' she dismissed with deliberate lightness, glad of that lightness as she saw Gareth's scowl deepen. 'Gareth—Patrick McGrath,' she added economically, still too shaken by that kiss to think how to describe him to the other man.

'*The* Patrick McGrath?' Gareth questioned abruptly as he looked frowningly at the other man.

Patrick smiled—a smile that didn't reach the cold grey of his eyes. 'I very much doubt there's only one Patrick McGrath in the world,' he answered the other man tauntingly.

'We really should be going in, Patrick,' Ellie put in determinedly as she saw the light of challenge that had now appeared in both men's eyes. 'If you'll excuse us, Gareth?' she added dismissively, not giving him a second glance as she turned and walked in the direction of the main restaurant, Patrick at her side, his arm still firmly about her waist.

Not quite the way she had envisaged the evening beginning!

But then she hadn't expected Patrick to kiss her either...

Why on earth *had* he kissed her? Just for effect, as his words afterwards had seemed to imply? Well, he couldn't even begin to imagine the effect his unexpected behaviour had had on her!

She could still feel the sensuous touch of his lips against hers, still feel the hardness of his body as she moulded perfectly against him, the warmth that had coursed through her, that totally not-knowing-where-she-was-and-not-caring-either feeling.

As for Gareth! Amazingly, she had felt absolutely nothing as she'd looked at him just now. Except perhaps a vague disbelief that she had ever been taken in by his overt good looks and charm...

What did it all mean...?

But as they walked into the restaurant and Patrick was greeted effusively by her boss, George Delacorte, Senior Partner at Delacorte, Delacorte and Delacorte, Ellie knew she would have to get back to that particularly puzzling question later!

CHAPTER THREE

'I HAD no idea you were going to be here with Ellie this evening, Patrick.' The older man greeted him warmly and the two men shook hands. George Delacorte was a tall, distinguished-looking man with iron-grey hair and twinkling brown eyes that belied the shrewd trial lawyer he actually was. 'You should have told me, Ellie,' he chided teasingly.

Told him what? Until a few seconds ago she hadn't even known that he and Patrick were acquainted! Patrick certainly hadn't mentioned that he knew the older man.

'How are Anne and Thomas?' George smiled.

'Very well, thank you, sir,' Patrick replied smoothly, his arm still lightly about Ellie's waist, almost as if he weren't aware that she was staring up at him in amazement.

Why hadn't he told her he knew George Delacorte? It was obvious from the easy way he was talking with the older man that Patrick had been perfectly well aware that he would be seeing the other man this evening! In fact, she knew that he had; she had told him herself that it was the Delacorte Christmas dinner!

'And Teresa?' the older man continued lightly. 'Breaking hearts, as usual?'

Patrick shrugged. 'I think she might finally have met ''the one'',' he answered indulgently.

'Good for her.' George chuckled.

Who on earth were Anne and Thomas—let alone Teresa? Ellie realised she really should have asked Patrick for a few more personal details. And maybe she would have done if she had known they would be relevant to this evening!

'I must just go and tell Mary you're here; she'll be so pleased to see you,' George said happily. 'Sarah is here too—somewhere.' He frowned. 'You're coming to the family party tomorrow?' he prompted abruptly.

'Of course,' Patrick assured him.

'Bring Ellie, too,' George went on with a smile in her direction. 'If you would like to come, my dear?' he added gently.

She had no idea what party either of these two men were talking about!

'I'm not sure what Ellie's plans are for tomorrow.' Patrick was the one to answer smoothly. 'We'll let you know.'

'Of course,' George accepted briskly. 'I'll just go and find Mary.' He gave them another smile before going off in search of his wife.

'So that was the infamous Gareth,' Patrick murmured thoughtfully once the two of them were alone. 'I have to say, Ellie, I wasn't very impressed.' He shrugged.

'Never mind Gareth for now—who are Anne, Thomas and Teresa?' Ellie hissed explosively. 'And how is it that you know George Delacorte?'

'He's my uncle,' Patrick told her dismissively, at the same time looking interestedly at the forty or so other Delacorte staff in the room. 'As for Anne, Thomas and—'

'Your uncle?' Ellie spluttered incredulously, gaping up at him unbelievingly.

'By marriage.' Patrick nodded. 'Mary Delacorte is my father's sister.'

'Why on earth didn't you tell me?' she demanded indignantly.

Patrick turned to look at her, dark brows raised over slightly mocking grey eyes. 'I didn't think it was relevant.'

'You-didn't-think-it-was-relevant!' she repeated disgustedly.

'Ellie, why do you keep repeating everything I say?' he taunted derisively.

'Because I just can't believe this!' The colour was high in her cheeks, blue eyes sparkling. 'Is Toby aware that my boss is your uncle?' she asked suspiciously as that idea suddenly occurred to her.

'I'm really not sure.' Patrick shrugged. 'But I would have thought so. Do you think we ought to mingle?' he added consideringly. 'Several of your work colleagues have looked curiously across at us in the last few minutes.'

She didn't care who had looked at them in the last few minutes; she intended getting to the bottom of this if it took all night. If Toby knew that Patrick was related to George Delacorte, then he must also be aware—

'Patrick!'

Ellie turned just in time to see Sarah Delacorte, George's daughter and only child, throw herself into Patrick's arms, kissing him enthusiastically.

Ellie felt her heart plummet as she looked at the

beautiful young woman laughing up into Patrick's face, her pleasure at his presence obvious.

Sarah Delacorte was beautiful, there was no doubt about that, with her tall, slender figure—shown off to advantage now in a slinky black knee-length dress—her long silky blonde hair and delicate child-like features.

Unfortunately she was also the woman Gareth had been dating for the last six weeks and was about to announce his engagement to!

And she was, Ellie realised with dismay, Patrick's young cousin…

'What are you doing here?' Sarah demanded, still holding onto Patrick's hands as she gazed up at him in obvious delight.

Patrick looked no less pleased to see his cousin, grinning broadly. 'Ellie brought me,' he explained lightly, releasing one of his hands to turn and firmly clasp one of Ellie's, to bring her forward to stand at his side.

'Goodness, Ellie, I haven't seen you for ages!' Sarah greeted her warmly. 'You look wonderful!' she added with genuine warmth.

It was true the two women hadn't met for some time. Sarah had been in Paris for the last year, initially working with one of the fashion designers over there. But her career in modelling had taken a meteoric rise over the last six months, with her photograph appearing on the front page of all the popular women's magazines.

Sarah's absence abroad was also the reason she had no idea Ellie had still been dating Gareth until six weeks ago!

Ellie very much doubted that Gareth had told the

other woman anything about her, or the fact that they had still been dating after he and Sarah met. And Ellie certainly had no intention of telling the other woman any of that either. Although the fact that she now knew Patrick was the other woman's cousin certainly made things more than a little awkward in that direction!

'I understand congratulations are in order?' Patrick looked down teasingly at his young cousin.

Ellie noted that the warmth was no longer in his eyes, and his smile lacked some of its earlier spontaneity...

'Isn't it wonderful?' Sarah said dreamily, suddenly looking a very young twenty-one-year-old. 'One moment I was young and fancy-free, and the next—I was just swept off my feet the moment I looked at him!' She laughed self-consciously.

Patrick's hand tightened about Ellie's fingers as he felt her stiffen beside him, although his narrowed gaze remained fixed on his cousin's glowingly lovely face. 'Love at first sight, hmm?' he prompted dryly.

'Something like that.' Sarah gave another happy laugh. 'Wait until you meet him,' she enthused. 'You're going to love him!'

Considering what Patrick had said to Ellie about Gareth a few minutes earlier, she somehow doubted that very much!

Although how much of Patrick's opinion had been formed by what Ellie might have said or implied about the other man and what Patrick had actually decided for himself she had no idea!

Not that it mattered; this was just a very awkward situation all round.

What on earth had Toby been playing at when he

originally organised this date for her with Patrick? Because Toby, of all of them, was well aware of the connection of all the key players in what was turning out to be a fiasco!

Patrick gave a slight inclination of his head. 'I'm sure you'll have a chance to introduce the two of us later. For the moment, I think Ellie wants to introduce me to some of her friends,' he added lightly.

'Of course,' Sarah instantly accepted. 'It really is lovely to see you again, Ellie,' she added warmly. 'We must go out and have coffee together some time, like we used to.'

When Sarah, no doubt, would want to wax lyrical about Gareth! No, thank you!

It was true the two women had occasionally had coffee together before Sarah's departure for Paris, but they had lost touch with each other during the last year. In the present circumstances Ellie thought it better if it remained that way!

'We must,' Ellie agreed non-committally.

'Catch up with you later, Sarah,' Patrick told his cousin, before strolling away, Ellie very firmly pinned to his side. 'Save it for later, hmm?' he told her between barely moving lips.

'But—'

'Ellie, this is not the place to discuss it. Okay?' he prompted as she came to an abrupt halt in the middle of the crowded room.

No, it was not okay. She had no idea what was going on—how could she when the whole evening had been turned upside down by Patrick's family connection to the Delacortes?

He sighed at the mutinous expression on her face. 'I know how this must look to you—'

'You can have no *idea* how this looks to me,' she assured him derisively.

'Probably not,' Patrick conceded with a grimace. 'But we do have the rest of this evening to get through,' he reasoned. 'And your ex-boyfriend's engagement is still going to be announced before the end of it.'

'Gareth's engagement to *your cousin*,' Ellie bit out pointedly.

'Yes,' he acknowledged heavily. 'It probably escaped your notice earlier, but George isn't exactly thrilled at the prospect of having Gareth Davies as his son-in-law!'

Ellie blinked. 'He isn't?'

Of course George had known that Ellie was dating Gareth until a couple of months ago—everyone at Delacorte, Delacorte and Delacorte had been aware of it. But when the older man had approached the subject of Sarah's involvement with the other man with Ellie she had dismissed her own relationship with him as a mere friendship. After all, she did have her pride...

She hadn't realised that George was talking to her about Gareth because he didn't exactly trust the younger man's motives regarding his daughter!

'No,' Patrick confirmed grimly.

She frowned. 'Then why doesn't he do something about it?'

Patrick smile derisively. 'Such as what? Tell Sarah he's nothing but a fortune-hunter? Because he is, isn't he?' he drawled scathingly. 'A man with an eye to the main chance. A man who fancies the name Davies being added to the end of Delacorte, Delacorte and Delacorte!'

Yes, that was exactly what Gareth was. Handsome, charming—but totally mercenary. Ellie, as George's much-valued secretary, had seemed like a good prospect to him six months ago. But Gareth had dropped her like a hot coal when Sarah had returned from Paris and he'd realised George had a marriageable daughter.

'Yes,' Ellie confirmed miserably, feeling totally humiliated by her own past gullibility.

Patrick nodded abruptly. 'And how do you think Sarah is likely to react if anyone should tell her that about the man she believes herself madly in love with?'

How would Ellie have reacted if someone had told her those things about Gareth three months ago? Even two months ago? Would she have believed them if she weren't now the one with the knowledge of just how mercenary Gareth could be?

She gave a derisive grimace. 'She'll tell them to mind their own business!'

'In one.' Patrick nodded in mocking confirmation.

Ellie shook her head dismissively. 'But if George really distrusts his motives—'

'He does,' Patrick bit out grimly.

'Then why doesn't he just sack him?'

'For the same reason, wouldn't you think?' Patrick derided.

Yes, Ellie *did* think. It was obvious from Sarah's behaviour earlier, from the things she had said about Gareth, that the other woman was completely taken in by him.

As Ellie had once been...

But, as Ellie had learnt only too well—and obviously Patrick and his uncle knew too—Gareth's charm was all a front for his calculating brain, to create Delacorte, Delacorte, Delacorte, and Davies!

At only thirty-two Gareth had ambitions that he had no intention of working at if they could be achieved by a simpler route—such as marrying the senior partner's daughter!

It had taken Ellie almost two weeks to realise that Gareth was dating someone else besides herself—he hadn't wanted to give up on one option before making absolutely sure of the second one! Once she had realised what he was doing she had told him precisely what she thought of him. And what he could do with the relationship he had tried to offer her as consolation prize.

If she had thought he was genuinely in love with Sarah then it would have been a different matter; she would have just accepted the inevitable. But by that time her eyes had been wide open where Gareth was concerned, her illusions shattered.

But she still had no idea what Patrick was up to...

Because he was up to something. She was sure of it!

'So, Ellie, what do you think?' Patrick looked at her consideringly now. 'Do you want to help us prove to Sarah what an absolute bas—What a calculating mercenary her new fiancé actually is?' he amended harshly.

Ellie glanced across the room to where she could see Gareth, now talking to Sarah, a superior smile curving his lips as she looked up at him with absolute adoration, obviously enthralled by his every word.

A shudder ran down Ellie's spine. Had she once

looked and felt as Sarah so obviously did? She had been attracted to Gareth, of that she had no doubt—just as she had no doubt that she had been meant to feel attracted to him! She had been flattered by his interest too—what woman wouldn't be when he was so handsome and charming? But she was relieved to realise that if she had ever believed herself in love with him it had been short lived, because she felt nothing but disgust as she looked at him now.

She turned back to Patrick, her shoulders straightening with resolve. 'I have absolutely no idea how you intend going about that, but, yes, I'm willing to help. If I can,' she added uncertainly.

If Patrick and George, two very capable men, had no idea how to go about revealing Gareth in his true colours to the besotted Sarah, what could she possibly do to achieve that?

Simply telling Sarah what she thought of Gareth would do no good. She had thought of that once she'd become aware that Sarah was Gareth's latest target— her concern and liking for Sarah were completely genuine—but she had concluded that Sarah was very unlikely to believe anything she had to say about Gareth once he had told Sarah the 'woman scorned' story. Pity was the more probable emotion Sarah would feel on hearing it—for Ellie!

Patrick gave her hand a triumphant squeeze. 'I hoped my instinct about you was right, Ellie,' he told her warmly.

She eyed him uncertainly. 'What instinct?'

He grinned. 'I knew you were a fighter,' he said with satisfaction. 'You had to be, to have chosen and succeeded in taking on the responsibilities you did eight years ago. Any woman who could do that isn't going to let a man like Gareth Davies get away with any-thing—least of all gulling some other poor woman in the same way you were!'

Again, Ellie was sure there was a compliment in there somewhere—it was just buried beneath the insult that had followed it!

CHAPTER FOUR

'WHAT on earth do you think you're playing at?'

Ellie turned slowly to face Gareth, already knowing by the aggressive tone of his voice that his mood was ugly. She had briefly left the dinner table after dessert to go to the ladies' room. Gareth must have deliberately followed her.

Yes, she was right about Gareth's mood. He looked less than handsome in his anger, blue eyes glittering furiously as he strode purposefully towards her.

'I'm sorry?' she answered coolly, very aware of the fact they were completely alone in the foyer. The receptionist was inside, helping to serve drinks now, the Delacorte party having taken over the whole restaurant for the evening.

'You heard me, Ellie,' he snapped impatiently. 'What are you doing here with George's nephew?'

'Eating dinner, the same as everyone else,' she dismissed with a lightness she was far from feeling. She knew that physically there was nothing Gareth could do to her here—even if he did look as if he would like to wring her neck—but verbally he could rip her to shreds!

Gareth's mouth twisted frustratedly. 'Don't get clever with me, Ellie,' he scorned. 'Moving in rather exalted company nowadays, aren't you?' he added insultingly.

Deliberately so, Ellie knew. Although she refused to become angry. Or at least only with herself—that she could ever have been taken in by such a man. In fact, it was a pity Sarah couldn't see him in this mood—the younger woman would have no doubts about his duplicitous charms then!

But Ellie knew what he was referring to with that remark about 'exalted company'; ordinarily she would have been seated at one of the tables with other secretaries and their partners, but as the nephew of the senior partner was her guest for the evening, she and Patrick had been moved onto the top table with the other senior members of staff.

The same table as Gareth and Sarah...

Ellie coolly met Gareth's accusing gaze. 'Do you have some sort of problem with that?'

He gave a scornful laugh. 'Not at all. So if you were hoping to make me jealous—'

'Don't flatter yourself, Gareth!' she cut in derisively, feeling her anger starting to rise. Really, the conceit of the man...! 'The fact that Patrick and I are—friends has absolutely nothing to do with you.'

'Have you said anything to him about me?' Gareth rasped nastily, taking a painful grip of her arm. 'Because if you have—'

'Gareth, believe me, when I'm with Patrick I have better things to do with my time than discuss you,' she assured him hardly. 'Now, would you kindly let go of my arm?' she asked coldly.

He looked down at her with hard blue eyes, a humourless smile now curving his lips. 'No, I don't think I will,' he murmured slowly. 'You're looking rather beautiful tonight, Ellie,' he told her huskily. 'Rather sexy, in fact.'

Nausea welled up in her throat at this completely unwelcome compliment from a man she now despised, but the coldness of her gaze didn't waver from his. 'Patrick happens to like me in red,' she told him challengingly.

The angry glitter intensified in Gareth's eyes. 'Why, you little—'

'Everything all right, darling?' Patrick's voice suddenly interrupted pleasantly. 'You've been gone so long I thought there must be something wrong?' he added questioningly, and he strolled over to join them, much to Ellie's relief. She instantly felt the reassurance of his presence.

Gareth slowly released her arm, and Ellie resisted the impulse she had to wipe his touch from her flesh. Instead she shot Gareth a look of intense dislike before turning to smile her gratitude at Patrick. 'I was just directing Gareth to the men's room,' she dismissed lightly.

'Really?' Patrick turned cold grey eyes on the younger man. 'But I thought that was where you were going when we met earlier this evening?'

Gareth pulled himself together with obvious effort, even managing to give the other man a rueful smile. 'Actually, I was collecting Sarah's wrap that time,' he explained pleasantly.

No doubt Gareth was making an effort to be pleasant because he was very aware that Patrick was George's nephew, Ellie guessed shrewdly.

'Ah, yes. My cousin Sarah.' Patrick murmured coldly. 'I'm very fond of Sarah,' he added softly.

'She's a marvellous girl,' Gareth agreed heartily.

'That she is,' Patrick acknowledged evenly. 'I would hate to see her hurt in any way,' he added softly, a dangerous stillness surrounding him.

Ellie was watching Gareth as Patrick made this remark. The handsome face remained pleasantly smiling, but there was a certain wariness in the younger man's eyes.

She wasn't sure it was absolutely wise for Patrick to challenge the other man, even in this mild way—not when his cousin's happiness was at stake. But, as she was quickly learning, Patrick really did like to do things his own way.

Gareth gave an inclination of his head. 'We really should be getting back; George is going to announce our engagement as soon as the coffee has been served.'

'So I believe,' Patrick rasped, once again holding tightly to Ellie's arm as he felt her stiffen. 'You go ahead,' he encouraged the other man. 'I just want to— have a few minutes alone with Ellie,' he drawled dryly.

'I was just telling Ellie that she's a bit of a dark horse,' Gareth drawled teasingly. 'Who knows, Ellie? We may even be related to each other one day!' he added mockingly.

How Ellie wanted to smack that confident smile off his handsome face!

But instead she felt cold common sense come over her as she answered him. 'Somehow I doubt that very much,' she told him scathingly.

'I do hope your intentions are honourable, Patrick.' Gareth's smile didn't reach the hard glitter of his eyes. 'I should warn you George is extremely fond of Ellie—

treats her almost like another daughter. He will not be happy if he thinks you're trifling with her affections!'

She really would hit him in a minute, common sense notwithstanding!

George Delacorte *was* fond of her, and had taken her slightly under his parental wing after her parents had died. Which was what made this situation so difficult now; she would hate any inaction on her part to contribute to the unhappiness of George's only child. But at the same time, as Patrick had already pointed out, what could any of them do about it?

Patrick gave a confident smile as he released Ellie's arm and put his own arm about the slenderness of her waist. 'I don't think Ellie was referring to our own relationship when she cast doubt on the two of you ever being related,' he assured the other man derisively.

Gareth's gaze narrowed assessingly on the older man. 'I really wouldn't pay too much attention to second-hand opinions, if I were you, Patrick—especially when those opinions are biased, as Ellie's undoubtedly are,' he added, with a pitying glance in her direction.

Ellie would have hit him then, if Patrick's hand hadn't moved from her waist to take a firm grip of her arm once more. Gareth was making her sound like some twisted, lovesick, scorned woman, out to hurt him in any way that she could!

'I make a point of always forming my own opinions concerning other people,' Patrick told the other man smoothly. 'Which is why I'm here with Ellie this evening,' he added softly.

Gareth nodded. 'I know how much Ellie hated the thought of coming here on her own tonight.'

Why, the condescending—

'I can assure you, that was never an option,' Patrick told the other man derisively, turning to smile at Ellie, the hard glitter in his eyes telling her of his own—controlled—anger. 'There are plenty of other men who would willingly have taken my place tonight,' he assured Gareth hardly.

'Of course,' Gareth agreed sceptically. 'Well, I really should be getting back,' he added lightly. 'It wouldn't do for one half of the engaged couple not to be in the room when the announcement is made, now, would it?' He smiled before walking confidently back into the restaurant.

Ellie let out a deep breath, unaware until that moment that she had actually been holding it. The last few minutes had told her that Gareth was even more dangerous than she had thought he was. His vindictiveness where she was concerned was more than obvious—to the point that he had deliberately tried to belittle her in front of Patrick, to make her sound like a—

'Don't let him get to you, Ellie.' Patrick was looking down at her concernedly. 'He only behaved in the way he did because he's still not quite sure how much you've told me about him,' he added hardly.

Her main emotion at this moment was embarrassment. That she had been fooled by Gareth in the first place. That Patrick knew she had been fooled by him!

Because Patrick's opinion was important to her. And that had nothing to do with that pride she had been so desperately trying to hang onto for the last six weeks and everything to do with the fact that she did not want

Patrick to think of her as some poor, wounded woman, still in love with Gareth Davies.

Which, in turn, led her to wonder *why* Patrick's opinion of her was so important...

She gave a dismissive shake of her head; she couldn't think about that right now—had other things to deal with. 'I think Gareth could be a very dangerous man,' she said slowly.

'Not dangerous,' Patrick dismissed confidently. 'Irritating, yes. Extremely so as far as George is concerned. But I was watching Gareth Davies through dinner—and whenever he thought no one else was taking any notice he was watching you. The fact that he saw you go out of the room and followed you shows that he isn't quite as confident of the situation as he would like us to think he is,' he added shrewdly.

Ellie eyed him uncertainly. 'He isn't?' Gareth had seemed extremely confident to her! She hadn't been aware of the other man watching her as they all ate dinner either. But obviously Patrick had...

Patrick gave a slow shake of his head. 'You obviously bother Gareth Davies very much.'

'Somehow I doubt that,' she scorned disbelievingly.

'Oh, yes, you bother him, Ellie. At least, your being with me, Sarah's cousin, bothers him,' Patrick muttered, obviously deep in thought. 'In fact, we may not have to do anything other than produce you on a regular basis,' he added shrewdly.

Her eyes widened. 'What do you mean?'

Patrick grinned. 'You have him rattled, Ellie!' he said with satisfaction. 'All we have to do is keep up the pressure.'

Ellie wasn't sure she liked the sound of that! In exactly what way was Patrick proposing they 'keep up the pressure'...?

'Do you remember George mentioning a party earlier?' he reminded her.

'Tomorrow,' Ellie nodded slowly, eyeing him warily.

As far as she was concerned this evening was a one-off situation. Especially as it had turned out to be so much more complicated than she could ever have realised.

But Patrick seemed to have other ideas...

He nodded. 'The official engagement party.' He grimaced. 'I think it would be a good idea if you were to—'

'No,' Ellie cut in firmly, at the same time shaking her head in protest. 'The answer is no, Patrick,' she insisted determinedly as his expression turned cajoling. 'As far as I've been able to ascertain you accompanied me this evening under false pretences,' she told him accusingly. 'Admittedly you were doing me a favour, but as circumstances have turned out I think that favour has more than been returned. After all, George is your uncle; you knew that the engagement announcement I told you about was actually between Gareth and your cousin—that's why you weren't surprised when I arrived in your office earlier in the week!' Her eyes sparkled accusingly as that realisation finally dawned on her too.

'Ellie—'

'No, Patrick.' She firmly resisted his teasing tone. 'This evening has been awful. I have no wish to repeat it.'

'Awful, Ellie?' Patrick repeated softly, suddenly standing much closer than was comfortable. For her peace of mind! 'All of it?' he prompted huskily.

No, as it happened, not all of it. The kiss the two of them had shared earlier had been more pleasurable than she cared to think about. Certainly more disturbing than she cared to admit!

'All of it,' she insisted forcefully. 'I am absolutely, definitely not going to the party with you tomorrow!'

He looked at her consideringly. 'Not even for Sarah's sake?'

'Not even for— That's emotional blackmail, Patrick!' she snapped irritably as her resolve began to sway at the mention of Sarah.

She and Sarah had been good friends in the past, and she knew the other girl to be bubbly, loving, completely carefree. Marriage to Gareth, once Gareth had shown just how ruthless he could be—and there was no doubting that he *would* show himself in his true colours one day—promised to ruin all that.

'I don't want to go to this party with you, Patrick,' she protested.

And it sounded weak, even to her own ears.

'I have nothing to wear!' she added inconsequentially when he made no reply.

Which sounded even weaker!

As evidenced by the fact that Patrick laughed, eyes twinkling warmly, his teeth showing whitely in his mouth—that mouth that only two hours ago, on this very spot, had very thoroughly kissed hers!

It was a mistake to think of that kiss...

Because she wanted very badly for Patrick to repeat it!

Something of that desire must have shown in her face, because Patrick took her very firmly by the shoulders and held her away from him at arm's length. 'No, Ellie,' he murmured regretfully. 'I'm not going to be accused of seduction as well as emotional blackmail!' He grimaced.

Ellie felt warmth enter her cheeks at her emotions being that transparent. Maybe it was the way her gaze had gone to his mouth—and stayed there. Or maybe it was just an expression of longing on her face. Either way, it wasn't very sophisticated of her to allow her emotions to be so easily gauged.

'Very well, Patrick,' she bit out abruptly. 'I'll come to the party with you—'

'I knew you wouldn't let me down!' Patrick beamed, seeming to forget his resolve as he pulled her into his arms to hug her.

Ellie pulled back, looking up at him warningly. 'I'm not doing this for you,' she reminded him firmly.

'No, of course you aren't,' he accepted lightly, but he still grinned broadly, looking far too attractive for Ellie's peace of mind. For the sudden rapid beat of her heart. For the heated longing that coursed through her body. For the way she wanted to just throw caution to the winds and kiss him if he wasn't about to kiss her!

She really would have to get a grip on her emotions where Patrick McGrath was concerned. Because to fall in love with him wouldn't only be ill-advised—it would be pure madness!

CHAPTER FIVE

'NOT a word,' Ellie cautioned Toby when he looked up from reading the Saturday newspaper as she came into the kitchen, dressed warmly for going out, needing only to pull her coat on when the time came. 'Not one word, Toby,' she repeated as he continued to look at her. 'You aren't my favourite person at the moment,' she added, and dropped down onto one of the kitchen chairs to wait.

Toby returned her gaze with too-innocent blue eyes. 'I can't imagine why you're in such a bad mood, sis.' He shrugged unconcernedly. 'You know how you love shopping.'

Ordinarily she did. But today wasn't ordinary. As Toby very well knew.

She glared across the table at her brother. 'I think working for Patrick is having a bad effect on you,' she muttered bad-temperedly. 'You're becoming as sneaky as he is!'

Toby chuckled softly. 'You forgot ''underhand'', ''secretive'', and—''manipulative'', wasn't it?' he prompted lightly.

They were all the names she had called her brother this morning, after he had asked her how the previous evening had gone!

'You forgot ''too clever for your own good'',' she reminded him heavily, but her mood began to thaw slightly. 'You really should have told me, Toby.' She shook her head disgustedly.

'But then you wouldn't have gone to the dinner last night. At least, not with Patrick,' he reasoned. 'And that would have been a pity.'

Ellie eyed him suspiciously. 'Why?'

'Hey, look, Ellie, in case you've forgotten Patrick and I are two of the good guys,' Toby pointed out protestingly. 'Gareth is the bad guy—remember?'

Oh, yes, she remembered. She also remembered that look of triumph on Gareth's face the previous evening when George had stood up to announce the younger man's engagement to his daughter, Sarah.

'He doesn't deserve Sarah, Ellie—let alone you!' Patrick had muttered disgustedly at her side.

Which was why, when the Delacorte family—and Ellie—had all been chatting together at the end of the evening, Patrick had been only to happy to suggest that Ellie accompany Sarah the following day, when she shopped for a new dress to wear to the party tomorrow evening!

'Ellie has just been complaining that she has nothing to wear either,' Patrick had told his young cousin happily.

Ellie glared up at him; she might have said something along those lines, but as Patrick must know only too well Sarah was the last person she wanted to go shopping with.

'I don't mind coming with you, Sarah,' Gareth put in—rather hastily, it seemed to Ellie. A brief glance at Patrick, his expression knowingly satisfied, showed her that he thought so too.

'It's very sweet of you, darling.' Sarah gave her new fiancé's arm a grateful hug, the emerald and diamond engagement ring twinkling brightly on her left hand. 'But you know how you hate shopping. Besides, I want the dress I'm wearing tomorrow evening to be a surprise.'

'I thought it was the wedding dress I wasn't supposed to see until the day?' Gareth frowned.

'It is, silly.' Sarah laughed huskily. 'I just—wait and see,' she dismissed excitedly, before turning to Ellie. 'I think it would be lovely for the two of us to go shopping together tomorrow, don't you?'

It was obvious from Sarah's completely confident expression that she didn't expect Ellie to refuse. And, with Patrick looking at Ellie with the same expectation, what choice did she have? Absolutely none.

Which was why she was sitting here now, dressed warmly in jeans and a thick sweater, waiting for Sarah to pick her up so they could drive into town together.

'I remember,' she answered Toby heavily. 'Until Patrick told me last night I had no idea how worried George and Mary are by the relationship.' She shook her head.

'Strange how these things come around in circles, isn't it?' Toby said ruefully. 'Your dastardly ex-boyfriend engaged to Patrick's cousin,' he explained, at Ellie's questioning look.

Ellie winced at having Gareth described as her ex-boyfriend; she just wanted to forget she had ever known him. Which was impossible in the present situation.

Although she had felt slightly warmed by Patrick's comment last night— 'He doesn't deserve Sarah,

Ellie—let alone you!' Quite what he had meant by that she wasn't sure, but again it had sounded as if there might be a compliment in there somewhere.

A compliment she would be wise to ignore, if she had any sense. And, after her recent disappointment over Gareth, she ought to have a lot of sense!

Except...

She had felt quite shy as Patrick had driven her home last night, wondering exactly how they were going to say goodnight to each other. Not that they had been out on a genuine date or anything—even less so than she had initially realised!—but Patrick *had* kissed her earlier in the evening.

She hadn't known whether to be disappointed or relieved when, having walked her to the door, he'd bent to kiss her lightly on the cheek before telling her he would call for her at eight o'clock the following evening.

'There's no point in getting there too early,' he had added grimly.

'None at all,' she agreed with a grimace.

'And don't worry about the shopping expedition with Sarah tomorrow,' he told her with a grin. 'Just be yourself and nothing can go wrong.'

Which was okay for Patrick to say—but Ellie did not relish the thought of having to listen to several hours of Sarah telling her how wonderful Gareth was. It promised to be a very trying afternoon.

'Buy something blue, Ellie,' Patrick had added huskily. 'The same blue as your eyes.'

Once again Ellie felt warmed by the fact that he had even noticed what colour her eyes were!

'Oh, and by the way—' he turned before getting into his car '—Anne and Thomas are my parents; Teresa's my younger sister.'

Oh, great. She was going to meet all of Patrick's family tomorrow evening, too.

'That dress is perfect on you, Ellie,' Sarah told her admiringly as Ellie came out of the changing room.

It might be, but a brief glance at the label whilst in the changing room had shown Ellie that the price was perfect too—for bankrupting her!

She should have known the other woman would want to go to a designer shop for her own outfit. In fact, Sarah had already picked out a gown—an emerald-green sheath that perfectly matched the emerald in her engagement ring—and had only returned to try the dress on after alterations.

The dress she had persuaded Ellie to try on was indeed the blue that Patrick had suggested, its material pure silk, with a fitted, mandarin-style collar and short sleeves.

'With your dark hair swept up like it was last night, and some kohl around your eyes, you'll look positively exotic, Ellie,' Sarah enthused.

The gown was beautiful, it was also more glamorous than anything Ellie had ever worn before. Dared she buy it?

'Patrick is going to be bowled over when he sees you in this,' Sarah added encouragingly.

She wasn't sure she wanted Patrick 'bowled over' when he saw her. Where could any relationship between the two of them ever go? Nowhere, came the resounding answer. And yet a part of her so wanted the dress—if only to see if she *could* bowl Patrick over...!

'Why don't you think about it while the two of us have a cup of coffee?' Sarah proposed as she saw Ellie's uncertainty.

'Good idea,' Ellie accepted with a certain amount of relief.

Although she wasn't so sure it *had* been a good idea once the two women were seated in a coffee-shop further down the street and the conversation naturally turned to Sarah's engagement!

'It was all a bit—sudden, wasn't it?' Ellie suggested lightly as she stirred sweetener into her coffee.

'Mmm,' Sarah acknowledged thoughtfully. 'I've quite enjoyed this last year—the modelling and having my photograph on the cover of magazines but you know, Ellie, it's a very lonely sort of life too. I missed my friends, the family,' she added wistfully. 'Most of all the family. Marriage, the possibility of having my own family, suddenly seemed the right option.'

But, as Ellie knew only too well, Gareth most certainly wasn't the right man to share that option!

'You're only twenty-one, Sarah,' she teased. 'There's plenty of time for that once you've done all the other things you want to do with your life. Didn't you once mention that you wanted to do some fashion designing of your own?'

'I've already done some,' Sarah told her excitedly. 'I had totally forgotten in the excitement of the last few weeks,' she went on ruefully, 'but I'm waiting for Jacques, the designer I worked with in Paris, to tell me what he thinks of them.'

Ah. So Sarah hadn't completely given up on her life in Paris after all...

'That sounds interesting,' Ellie encouraged. 'Do you think that will affect your engagement to Gareth?'

Sarah looked startled. 'I must admit I hadn't given that much thought.' She grimaced. 'This being engaged and having to think of another person is all new to me,' she added self-derisively. 'But I would really like to follow it through if Jacques thinks I have any talent at all.'

Again, this was encouraging, Ellie thought; it showed the other woman wasn't yet quite so tied up in her relationship with Gareth that she had given up on her own ambitions.

'I'm sure Gareth will understand if we have to wait a while before getting married,' Sarah added dismissively.

Ellie thought the other woman was being slightly optimistic concerning Gareth's patience in that direction— after all, the sooner Sarah was his wife, the sooner his position at Delacorte, Delacorte and Delacorte was secured—but wisely she didn't voice any of those doubts to Sarah.

She did, however, relay the conversation to Patrick when he arrived to collect her that evening.

'You look wonderful, Ellie.' He stood back to look at her appreciatively.

Ellie felt warmth in her cheeks at his praise. 'Patrick, didn't you hear what I said? Sarah—'

'Still has plans to become a fashion designer,' he finished dismissively. 'That's great. But—'

'Just ''great''?' Ellie persisted frowningly. 'Don't

you realise this could be the way to drive a rift between her and Gareth?'

'Well, of course I realise that,' he confirmed lightly. 'He isn't going to like the idea of a delayed marriage at all.'

'Exactly,' Ellie said with satisfaction. 'Which is good—isn't it…?' she added uncertainly when Patrick didn't look as thrilled by the news as she had been earlier.

'Very good.' He nodded. 'But at the moment I'm more interested in the way you look, Ellie. That dress is—you look wonderful,' he said again.

Ellie had given in to impulse and gone back to the shop to buy the blue silk gown, aware that it was costing a small fortune but for the moment not caring. She had also swept up her hair and applied kohl to her eyes, as Sarah had suggested. The finished effect was pretty good, even if she did say so herself. And it was also good that Patrick liked the way she looked this evening. Wasn't it…?

That was the particular problem she had at the moment. There was no denying that she was attracted to Patrick, that she more than liked being in his company, but at the same time she was still very much aware that their relationship was nothing but a sham. It certainly wouldn't do for either of them to forget that. Because once this situation had been sorted out she and Patrick would go back to being strangers—perhaps occasionally mentioned to each other by Toby, but other than that strangers.

The fact that Patrick was once again dressed in evening clothes, and it made her heart flutter just to look at him, was not something Ellie could allow herself to dwell on!

There was also the matter of the large flat white box he had carried in under his arm...

'You told me off yesterday evening for repeating things,' she reminded him dryly.

'Telling you how beautiful you look in that dress deserves to be repeated,' he said unrepentantly, his gaze still appreciative. 'It's blue too,' he added with satisfaction.

'Shouldn't we be going?' Ellie prompted sharply, after a glance at her wristwatch, not particularly wanting to get into a conversation about why she had chosen this particular gown. 'After all, there's politely late and then there's just bad manners!'

Patrick laughed softly. 'You sound like my mother!'

Great! Just the person she wanted to be likened to!

'Oh, no, you don't.' Patrick removed the heavy winter coat from her hand as she would have put it on, throwing it back over a chair before laying the white box on the kitchen table and removing the lid. 'I bought you a present today,' he told her lightly, folding back the tissue paper in the box.

'A present?' Ellie gaped. 'For me? But—'

'For you,' Patrick repeated firmly, taking something black and woollen out of the box. 'It's a pashmina. It's made from the soft wool of goats in Northern India—'

'I know what it's made from,' Ellie cut in dazedly, staring at the soft woollen shawl. She also knew that it was very expensive! 'Patrick, you really shouldn't have—'

'I really should,' he told her firmly, shaking out the long shawl to drape it decorously about her shoulders. 'You deserve something in the way of thanks for what you're doing. Think of it as an early Christmas present. Besides,' he added as she would have protested again, 'that black coat does absolutely nothing for you,' he told her dryly.

Or for the image of the woman who was to be his partner for the evening, Ellie realized ruefully.

Not that he wasn't right about her long black winter coat; it had been bought more for warmth rather than as any sort of fashion statement. It was just the fact of Patrick having bought her a gift—an expensive one at that—that was so disturbing. And it might be Christmas in just over a week's time, but Patrick wouldn't have been buying her a present anyway...

But the shawl did feel so warm, and it had such panache—its front drape fell to just above her knees; the other drape was thrown stylishly across one shoulder by Patrick. She didn't want to refuse it!

Patrick's hands moved up to cradle either side of her face as he looked down at her intently. 'Just say, "Thank you, Patrick", politely,' he told her dryly. 'Give me a kiss for good measure. And then we'll be on our way.'

She tried to swallow, knowing which part of those instructions had suddenly caused this obstruction in her throat. Verbally thanking him would be no problem -

'Too difficult?' he teased mockingly. 'Okay, just kiss me and we'll forget all about saying thank you!'

That was the part that was bothering her! And Patrick knew it too. The light of challenge burned in those otherwise enigmatic grey eyes.

The problem was, if she 'just' kissed him, as he suggested, would either of them be able to forget about that? Ellie knew that she wouldn't!

'Don't take too long deciding, Ellie,' Patrick told her dryly. 'Or the party will be over before we even get there!'

Which, to Ellie's mind, wouldn't be a bad thing!

But she was prevaricating. She knew she was. Patrick knew she was, too. Why not just kiss him and get it over with?

'Thank you for my present, Patrick.' She stood on tiptoe and kissed him lightly on the mouth. 'But you shouldn't have—'

Patrick put silencing fingertips over her lips. 'Don't ruin it, Ellie,' he told her huskily. 'And do you call that a kiss?' he added derisively. 'Sarah shows me more enthusiasm than you just did!'

Sarah was his cousin, and perfectly free to kiss him as enthusiastically as she chose. Ellie—who wasn't quite sure what she was to him—felt rather more constrained.

'How about you try again, hmm?' Patrick encouraged throatily.

He was suddenly very close. Ellie was able to feel the warmth of his body, smell his spicy aftershave, and as she looked up into his eyes she could see that his pupils were dilated, so that only a ring of grey showed about the eyes.

'Patrick…!' She groaned huskily, before she once again rose on tiptoe, her mouth soft and pliant against his as she kissed him with all the pent-up longing inside her.

Patrick's arms moved about her waist as he pulled her in against his body, although he let Ellie continue to control the kiss.

If you could call it control when she just wanted to melt against him and give in to the languorous yearning of her body!

'Wow!' he breathed slowly when Ellie broke the kiss, lightly resting his forehead against hers. 'Now, that's what I call a kiss. You have hidden talents, Miss Fairfax,' he added warmly.

Ellie swallowed hard. 'I—'

'Will I do?' Toby burst unceremoniously into the kitchen, coming to an abrupt halt as he saw how close Ellie and Patrick were standing to each other. 'Sorry.' He grimaced self-consciously. 'I had no idea— I mean—'

'You'll do, Toby,' the older man told him dryly as he stepped away from Ellie. 'I was just telling your sister how beautiful she looks this evening,' he prompted pointedly.

'Er—yes, sis, you look great,' Toby said, a perplexed frown on his brow. He still sounded slightly flustered— as well he might; the last thing he had expected was to see Ellie and Patrick in what must have looked like a clinch!

Ellie was a little puzzled as to why Toby was dressed in a black dinner suit and white shirt...

Patrick shot the younger man a searching look, and whatever he saw there in Toby's face caused him to give an impatient shake of his head. 'Did I forget to mention that Toby is coming with us this evening?' he said blandly, turning to pick up his car keys from where he had left them on the table earlier.

Not only had he forgotten to mention it—but so had Toby!

CHAPTER SIX

ELLIE still had no idea, seated beside Patrick in the front of the car as he drove competently through the busy streets, why her brother should be accompanying them.

Obviously he was Patrick's assistant, but this was a family party, to celebrate—or commiserate!—with Sarah on her engagement to Gareth. Admittedly, Toby obviously knew much more of the Delacorte family than Ellie had at first realised, but what possible place did he have amongst such a gathering?

She gave a dismissive shake of her head, giving up on trying to work that one out; she already had enough to think about this evening without worrying about why her brother should have been invited too.

Patrick's present, for one thing...

Even now Ellie snuggled down into the warmth of the shawl, loving the feel of the soft wool against her arms. And Patrick had obviously been out and bought the gift himself. Which made it doubly precious.

That kiss, for another thing...

Given enough opportunity, she could quite get used to kissing Patrick. In fact, she couldn't think of anything she enjoyed more, could still feel the sensuous warmth of his lips against hers...

Stop it, she instantly ordered herself exasperatedly. There was no point in getting used to Patrick kissing her. In fact, it might never happen again, so she had better get used to that!

The Delacorte house was ablaze with lights as Patrick parked the car outside. Over twenty cars were already parked in the long driveway—Jaguars, Mercedes, Rolls Royces and the occasional Range Rover, Ellie noted with a self-conscious grimace.

As Gareth had quickly realized when he'd come to work for Delacorte, Delacorte and Delacorte, Ellie was quite a favourite with George Delacorte, but she had never actually been to George and Mary's house before. She now found a butler opening the door to their ring, a maid taking their coats and wraps. The luxurious décor and furnishings of the house were all a bit overwhelming.

Did Patrick's parents have a house like this one too?

Probably, she acknowledged heavily. Even if, as she vaguely remembered Toby once telling her, as a bachelor of thirty-eight Patrick lived in an apartment of his own in town.

All this luxury made their own little house seem positively minute in comparison!

But then there was no point in comparison; the obvious wealth of Patrick's relatives only served to emphasise the differences between the two of them. Differences she would do well to remember.

There was the sound of voices and laughter coming from a sitting room that led off to the right of the huge reception hall, and it was to this room that Patrick took them, his hand lightly under Ellie's elbow. Almost as if he knew that what she really wanted to do was turn tail and run!

'My family doesn't bite, Ellie,' Patrick told her mockingly now. 'At least not on first acquaintance!' he added tauntingly.

'How reassuring,' Ellie drawled, taking a glass of champagne from the circulating waiter.

'If the two of you will excuse me…?' Toby muttered distractedly, before disappearing into the throng of people already crowded into the room.

Ellie watched his departure with puzzlement. 'What—?'

'Let's go and say hello to George and Mary,' Patrick suggested lightly. 'You had better hold my hand.' He held it out to her. 'I would hate to lose you in the crush.'

Ellie would hate to lose him too; she hadn't recognised a single face in the room so far, apart from George and Mary Delacorte where they stood over by the huge fireplace, chatting to another middle-aged couple.

It was undoubtedly a large room, seeming to run the entire width of the house, with a huge bay window at one end and doors out into the garden at the other, but with fifty or so people in it there was barely room to move.

'We have a large family,' Patrick told Ellie ruefully as he managed to push his way through in the direction of the fireplace.

Ellie and Toby had several aunts, uncles and cousins too, but they would be hard pushed to fill even their small sitting room with the dozen or so that made up their family.

It didn't help her nervousness when she instantly saw

the likeness between Mary Delacorte and the tall dark-haired man who made up half of the other couple the Delacortes were chatting to. She knew she was right in the conclusion she had come to as the man gave a light laugh; his likeness to Patrick was unmistakeable.

Saying good evening to George and Mary was one thing, meeting Patrick's parents was something else entirely!

Ellie came to an abrupt halt before they reached the foursome, giving Patrick an accusing glare when he looked down at her questioningly. 'I don't think that's a good idea, Patrick,' she bit out tautly.

He gave her a considering look. 'Ellie, introducing you to my parents is not tantamount to making a declaration about our relationship,' he finally drawled teasingly.

'No, Patrick.' She gave a firm shake of her head. 'Helping out with this situation concerning Gareth is one thing, but I won't complicate things by meeting your parents.' She determinedly released her hand from his. 'You go and say hello to them. I'll go and find the ladies' room.'

He frowned darkly. 'But—'

'I said no, Patrick.' Her gaze met his unwaveringly. 'I'll be standing over by the bay window when you've finished talking to them.'

'Wearing a pink carnation in your lapel?' he returned, with obvious impatience at her determination.

She gave the ghost of a smile. 'I don't have a lapel.'

Patrick shook his head as he looked down at her frustratedly. 'You are undoubtedly the most stubborn woman I've ever met!'

Her smile was more genuine this time. 'Nice to know I have the distinction of being something,' she returned unconcernedly.

His expression lightened. 'Oh, you're a lot more than that, Ellie,' he assured her dryly, before sighing resignedly. 'Okay, no introduction to my parents. But try not to get lost, hmm?' he encouraged.

As it happened, despite directions from the busy maid in the hallway, she did get lost—several times—and it was almost fifteen minutes later when she came back down the stairs. Only to walk straight into Gareth—literally—as he began walking up them.

The words of apology died on his lips as he looked up and recognised her. The boyish smile turned to one of derision. 'I thought you had decided not to come to the party after all when I saw your boyfriend was in there alone,' he bit out caustically.

Ellie straightened her shoulders, her hand tightly gripping her evening bag; Gareth was the last person she'd wanted to find herself alone with! 'Obviously you thought wrong,' she returned, non-committal—about the 'boyfriend' or the fact that she was there!

'Obviously,' Gareth acknowledged hardly. 'I don't know what you're hoping to achieve by all this, Ellie, but—'

'I have no idea what you're talking about,' she interrupted firmly, glancing over his shoulder in the hope that Patrick or Toby might see her predicament and come to her rescue; neither of them was in sight.

He grimaced. 'I realise that you're in love with me, Ellie, but—'

'You realise no such thing!' Ellie interrupted heatedly, knowing that briefly she might have thought herself in love with this man. But it had only been briefly. She was most certainly over whatever she had once felt for him! 'If I'm in love with anyone, it most certainly isn't you,' she added scathingly.

Gareth's gaze narrowed. 'McGrath?'

She didn't know what she felt for Patrick—had spent most of the last twenty-four hours determinedly not giving herself time to even think along those lines.

Her chin rose challengingly. 'And what if it is?'

He gave a pitying shake of his head. 'Then you're wasting your time there more than you were with me,' he scorned. 'Delusions of grandeur!' he added nastily.

'And what about you?' Ellie flushed angrily—more so because she knew what he said was true. 'Isn't Sarah Delacorte just as much out of your league as Patrick is out of mine?'

'Ah, but I've already succeeded with Sarah,' he reminded her confidently.

'Not for long, if I have my way,' Ellie snapped furiously. 'You— Let go of my arm, Gareth!' she gasped as he grasped her painfully on exactly the same spot he had the previous evening. And she had the bruises to prove it!

He ignored her, maintaining his grip, his face very close to hers now, his eyes glittering angrily. 'Don't try and mess this up for me, Ellie,' he warned softly. 'Because if you do—'

'Everything all right, Ellie?'

It was Toby who came to Ellie's rescue this time. Gareth released her in time for her to turn and see her brother strolling across the hallway to join them.

'Davies,' he greeted the other man coolly before turning to look at Ellie concernedly.

Ellie had a good idea what he would see too; she was both shocked and dismayed by Gareth's verbal attack on her, and the bruises on her arm were hurting.

'Ellie, Patrick was looking for you so that you can go into the buffet together,' Toby said softly. 'I think you should go and join him,' he added firmly.

She didn't want to rejoin Patrick; she just wanted to leave, to go home and lick her wounds—literally. Her arm really was throbbing, adding to the discomfort of the bruises already there.

'I'll just stay here and have a few quiet words with Gareth,' Toby continued lightly, before turning to the other man. 'I don't think I've congratulated you on your engagement yet, have I?'

Ellie left them to it. These confrontations with Gareth were unpleasant as well as nerve-shattering. Although Patrick seemed to be right in his surmise that she only needed to appear in order to upset Gareth's self-confidence. She just wasn't sure she was up to the effect these meetings were having on her own self-confidence!

Patrick was frowning darkly as she joined him by the window. 'Where on earth have you been?' he snapped. 'I finished talking to my parents long ago. I— What is it?' he probed concernedly when Ellie's eyes misted over with tears. 'Ellie…?' He lightly clasped her arm.

Ellie gasped at this added pressure on a spot that already felt black and blue, biting her bottom lip as her tears became tears of pain.

Patrick instantly released her when he realised he was

hurting her. 'Ellie, where have you been?' he asked slowly. 'And why does your arm hurt?'

She shook her head, desperately blinking back the tears; she didn't want to make a complete fool of herself—and Patrick—in front of his family. 'I bumped into Gareth in the hallway—'

'That's how you hurt your arm?' he ground out suspiciously, eyes narrowed to steely slits.

'Not exactly,' she conceded awkwardly. 'You see, I still have bruises there from last night, when he grabbed me, and—'

'Davies hurt you?' Patrick bit out, dangerously soft.

'I don't suppose he meant to,' she lied—knowing from the expression on Gareth's face earlier that he would greatly enjoy strangling her for what he saw as her interference! 'You see—'

'Yes, I do see, Ellie,' Patrick ground out harshly, his narrowed gaze searching as he looked across the room towards the door. 'Here's Toby,' he rasped. 'I want you to stay here with him—while I go and have a few words with my so-called future cousin-in-law!'

'Patrick, no—' But she was too late. He had already left her side, muttering a few words to her brother in passing before going out into the hallway himself.

This was awful! She deplored Sarah's choice of future husband, knew Gareth for exactly what he was, but the last thing Ellie wanted was to cause trouble at Sarah's engagement party. And she was pretty sure, from the grim expression on Patrick's face as he'd left her side, that there was going to be trouble!

Toby smiled as he reached her. 'Patrick wants me to

take you in to the buffet; he's going to join us in a few minutes.'

Maybe this was the reason Toby had accompanied them to the party—this way Patrick had ensured that she was never left alone. Except she had been...

'Toby, Patrick is going to find Gareth and, from the looks of him, hit him,' she said agitatedly, staring anxiously towards the direction in which Patrick had so recently disappeared.

'So?' Toby prompted unconcernedly.

'Toby—'

'Ellie,' he cut in firmly. 'I would have hit the man myself if I hadn't thought the bruises might show, but I had to settle for a few choice words instead. And talking of bruises...' He looked down at her searchingly. 'Patrick said something about Gareth having hurt you just now?'

She sighed her impatience, wishing she hadn't given away the fact that her arm was bruised beneath the sleeve of her dress. 'It doesn't matter,' she dismissed. 'What matters is that Patrick is going to make a scene.' Her eyes were wide with distress at the thought.

Toby gave a confident shake of his head. 'Patrick never makes a scene,' her brother assured her dryly.

No, he probably didn't—could probably get his point over by talking in that softly dangerous voice she had heard him use just now. But, nevertheless, she doubted Gareth would just meekly stand there and take whatever Patrick had to say to him.

'Come on, sis,' Toby encouraged lightly. 'Let's go through to the other room and get some food.'

The last thing Ellie felt like doing was eating! How

could she even think about food when Patrick and Gareth might even now be at each other's throats?

She hung back. 'I just want to go home, Toby.' She sighed. 'In fact, after tonight I need to rethink my whole life,' she added frowningly.

After tonight she wasn't even sure she could go on working in the same building with Gareth, let alone anything else. If Gareth could be this threatening in the midst of his future in-laws, what possible chance did she stand of avoiding his wrath at the office?

She had worked for Delacorte, Delacorte and Delacorte since leaving school at eighteen, had been steadily promoted through the firm, until she'd become George's personal secretary four years ago. It was a job she greatly enjoyed. At least, she had. The last couple of months, with the chance of bumping into Gareth around every corner, hadn't been quite so much fun. And after this evening it promised to get worse!

Toby frowned. 'I don't think you need to do anything drastic just yet, Ellie,' he cautioned. 'Give Patrick a bit more time to resolve the situation, hmm?'

She gave a wry smile. 'You have great confidence in your employer!'

Her brother gave a rueful shrug. 'I've never seen Patrick at the losing end of a fight yet.'

No, she could believe that; Patrick had the air of a man completely confident in his own abilities. But this situation was too personal, too close to home, to be dealt with like the business deals he was usually involved with.

'Hello, Ellie,' Sarah greeted her brightly, looking exceptionally beautiful in the green dress she had bought earlier that afternoon. 'You don't happen to have seen my fiancé about anywhere, do you?' she added ruefully.

Ellie felt the colour drain from her cheeks. 'Er—'

'He was outside talking to Patrick when I last saw him.' Toby was the one to answer. 'I'm Ellie's brother Toby, by the way,' he added lightly, holding out his hand in friendly greeting.

'Sarah Delacorte.' She gave Toby a considering look as she shook his hand. 'Yes, I can see the likeness.' She smiled warmly. 'You work with Patrick, don't you?'

'For him, actually,' Toby corrected dryly.

Sarah's smile widened. 'Of course. Well, it's very nice to meet you,' she added sincerely. 'I hope you'll both excuse me while I go and find Gareth?'

Ellie looked up impatiently at Toby once they were alone. 'Shouldn't you go and warn Patrick?'

Her brother shrugged unconcernedly. 'One thing I've learnt from working for Patrick—he's quite capable of taking care of himself. Now, let's go and get some food; I'm starving!' With his hand under her elbow he guided her through to the dining room.

Toby had learnt something else from working for Patrick, Ellie realized: how to take charge of a situation with the same arrogance!

Somewhere along the way, she realised dazedly as she put food on her plate without even noticing what she had chosen, her little brother had grown up...

She had spent so long thinking of him as her younger brother, that she just hadn't noticed him grow into a man almost as confident as the one he worked for.

He was a handsome man too, Ellie had to acknowledge as a girl of about twenty who stood helping herself to the buffet—probably yet another relative of Patrick's—gave him more than a cursory glance from beneath lowered dark lashes.

At twenty-six and over six feet tall, with short dark hair, laughing blue eyes, a pleasantly handsome face and a healthily fit body from his visits to the gym several times a week, her brother wasn't the boy she had always thought him; he was a man who was obviously attractive to women.

When had that happened? She—

'You aren't eating, Ellie.'

She turned sharply to find Patrick standing at her side, and quickly checked his face for signs of a fight. Thankfully she didn't find any.

'How was I supposed to eat when for all I knew you might have been lying unconscious in the hallway?' she came back, her sharpness due to her worry concerning his welfare.

Like a mother when her child came back to her unharmed after doing something she considered dangerous? Or like a woman worried about the man she loved…?

Patrick's reply didn't exactly calm her impatient anger. 'Not very likely,' he drawled confidently.

Ellie's eyes sparkled angrily. 'That's okay for you to say, but—'

'Ellie!' Toby cut in laughingly. 'I told you that Patrick is more than capable of taking care of himself.'

She glared at them both—Toby laughing, Patrick amused, one dark brow raised mockingly. 'Men!' she finally muttered frustratedly, turning away to pile more food haphazardly onto her plate.

'Are you sure you're going to eat all that?' Patrick murmured close beside her. 'Maybe we should just share the plate,' he added teasingly.

Ellie turned to find that she and Patrick were alone. Toby had wandered off, was now standing across the dining room chatting to the dark-haired girl who had given him such an admiring look a few minutes ago. He hadn't wasted much time!

She looked up at Patrick, some of her anger abating in the face of his teasing look. 'I had visions of a brawl in the hallway,' she admitted ruefully.

He shrugged. 'I very rarely resort to violence, Ellie. Although in Davies's case,' he added hardly, his expression becoming grim, 'I could be willing to make an exception. As it is, I've made it very clear what I will do to him if he so much as comes near you again, let alone touches you.'

Ellie raised dark brows. 'Oh?'

Patrick nodded abruptly. 'I think we need to discuss your continued involvement in all this.'

Ellie felt her heart stop for a moment. What did he mean? Was he suggesting that it was no longer necessary for her to be involved?

She might have decided minutes ago that she needed to rethink her life, to perhaps consider giving up her position at Delacorte, Delacorte and Delacorte as a way of avoiding accidentally bumping into Gareth any more. But she hadn't included not seeing Patrick any more in that rethinking... The very thought of that filled her with desolation.

A week ago Patrick had just been her brother Toby's boss—a man she had once shared an embarrassing experience with—but he was now so much more than that. How much more she still didn't want to admit to herself. She just knew she couldn't bear the thought of not seeing Patrick again!

Her mouth tightened. 'You can manage without me now—is that it?' She was waspish in her disappointment.

'I didn't say that.' Patrick gave her a reproving look. 'I just think that it might be better for you—'

'I'll decide what's best for me, if you don't mind,' Ellie told him shortly. 'And while I can still be of any help in preventing Sarah making a terrible mistake I intend staying very much in Gareth's face!' she announced firmly—in complete contradiction of what she had decided minutes ago!

But the only way she could continue to see Patrick was to remain a thorn in Gareth's side.

And she very much wanted to continue seeing Patrick...

CHAPTER SEVEN

'I'M SORRY, how did you say Toby was getting home?'
Ellie yawned tiredly as Patrick drove her home a couple
of hours later.

He shrugged dismissively. 'Someone he met at the
party is driving him back later, I believe.'

Ellie would take a bet on it being that pretty dark-
haired girl who had looked at him so interestedly as
they stood at the buffet table; she certainly hadn't seen
much of her brother during the rest of the evening.

Oh, well, good luck to him, Ellie thought slightly
enviously. She had spent the whole evening with
Patrick glued to her side—but for completely the wrong
reason!

'I felt so sorry for George and Mary this evening.'
She sighed heavily. The older couple's unhappiness at
their daughter's choice of future husband had been perfectly obvious to Ellie as they'd looked at Sarah so
wistfully. She frowned. 'Does Sarah really have no idea
how they feel about Gareth?'

'George has voiced his—reservations concerning the
speed of the engagement.' Patrick grimaced. 'Anything
else is sure to just make her all the more determined to
have her own way.'

Ellie turned to smile at him in the semi-darkness of
the illuminated streets they were driving through. 'Runs
in the family, does it?' she teased.

He gave a slight smile. 'Something like that.'

She could believe it. They were certainly an attractive family, but stubbornness seemed to be one of their less endearing characteristics.

'Gareth is going to cling like a leech,' Ellie warned heavily.

Patrick's mouth tightened. 'I agree. He's a parasite.'

How embarrassing it was for her that she had been the previous woman taken in by Gareth's charm! In fact, she would rather not talk about Gareth at all.

'So what's the next move?' she prompted briskly.

'Dinner on Tuesday, I thought,' Patrick came back lightly.

Ellie turned to him frowningly. 'What's happening on Tuesday evening?'

'I just said—dinner,' he dismissed.

'Yes, but—what's it for?'

He shot her a sideways glance. 'So we don't starve?'

'Yes, but—'

'You're repeating yourself again, Ellie,' he mused teasingly. 'I'm inviting you out to dinner on Tuesday evening,' he explained lightly.

Ellie's frown deepened. 'But—'

'Ellie, will you or will you not have dinner with me on Tuesday evening?' Patrick cut in patiently.

'Well, of course. I've already told you I'll do everything I can to help—'

'This is dinner with me, Ellie.' He parked the car in the driveway and turned in his seat to look at her. 'No one else. Well…I suppose there will be other people in the restaurant. But they will have nothing to do with us. Have I made myself clear now?'

If she understood this correctly, Patrick had just invited her out on a date!

He gave a smile at her perplexed expression. 'I believe it's usual to invite your escort in for coffee at the end of the evening.'

Ellie was still so dazed by his invitation out to dinner on Tuesday that she did ask him in, getting out of the car to unlock the front door of the house and lead the way in to the kitchen.

'Leave that for a minute,' Patrick murmured softly, and he took the coffee pot out of her hand, turning her to face him. 'I want to see the bruises on your arms,' he told her grimly as he removed the wrap from her shoulders.

She felt the colour warm her cheeks as he turned the sleeves back on her dress. There was a huge thumbprint-size bruise on the front of each arm, one already turning a sickly yellow, the new one a blue-black. Ellie stood still as Patrick walked around to look at the back of her arm, hearing the angry hiss that followed.

'I should have hit him while I had the chance,' Patrick snapped angrily. 'Damn it—I've a good mind to go back to the party right now and hit him anyway!' he bit out harshly.

Ellie shook her head as she pulled the sleeves back down over her arms. 'He really isn't important.'

'No, he isn't,' Patrick agreed abruptly as he moved to stand beside her, his eyes gleaming metallic grey. 'But I have no intention of just standing by while he hurts you.'

She gave a self-derisive laugh. 'You're a little late in the day to prevent him doing that!'

Patrick stepped back, watching her with hooded eyes as she prepared the coffee. 'Did you love him very much?'

'Not at all,' she answered with complete honesty. 'Oh, I may have thought I did for a while. But I was just—flattered by his attention, I suppose. Believe it or not, he can be very charming when he wants to be.' Besides, she already knew that the way Patrick made her feel, just by being in the same room as her, was far deeper than anything she might have thought she felt for Gareth!

'I'm sure he can,' Patrick dismissed scathingly.

'No—really.' She gave a self-conscious laugh.

It was strangely intimate in the quiet of the kitchen— the muted light under the kitchen cupboards the only illumination, the only sound the drip, drip of the coffee percolator.

Patrick's eyes were mesmerizing now as he looked down at her, obliquely black, ringed with silver. 'Dinner on Tuesday?' he prompted huskily.

'Er—Well—Yes,' she agreed awkwardly, still unsure as to the reason for his invitation. 'Although—'

'Just a yes will do,' Patrick assured her mockingly, his arms moving lightly about her waist. 'I would like to see you relaxed and enjoying yourself for a change,' he added frowningly.

If he thought she was going to be relaxed in his company then he was mistaken! Although she *would* enjoy spending the evening with him. If she knew the reason for it...

But he was standing so close now she couldn't even think straight, let alone try to rationalise his dinner invitation. Her heart was beating erratically, her breathing shallow as she looked up into the handsome ruggedness of his face.

'You look extremely lovely tonight, Ellie,' he told her huskily.

'You said that earlier,' she reminded him breathlessly.

He smiled, his eyes crinkling warmly at the corners. 'Some things need to be repeated.' His hands linked at the base of her spine and he moulded her body lightly against his, his head bending slightly as his lips moved teasingly across hers.

She had forgotten to breathe again, felt as if time itself were standing still. Only her hands resting on the broadness of Patrick's shoulders prevented her from actually falling down.

'You have a very kissable mouth, Ellie Fairfax,' Patrick murmured huskily as he took little sips from her lips. 'A very sensuous neck,' he whispered as his lips moved down the silky column of her throat. 'Divine breasts—'

'I think perhaps you should stop there, Patrick, don't you?' Ellie moved awkwardly in his arms, very aware of the sudden pertness of those 'divine breasts', the nipples hard against the silky material of her dress.

He straightened, his head tilted to one side as he regarded her quizzically. 'Why do I get the impression you're an innocent?' he murmured ruefully.

'Probably because I am!' Ellie admitted uncomfortably as she extricated herself from his arms, at the same time looking up at him irritably. 'There's nothing wrong with that,' she added sharply.

Patrick's smile deepened. 'Did I say there was?'

'You looked as if there was,' she snapped defensively.

He shook his head, still smiling. 'I don't think so, Ellie.'

Well...okay, maybe he hadn't. But he certainly seemed surprised to meet a twenty-seven-year-old virgin!

Maybe it *was* odd at that; Ellie really wouldn't know. It wasn't something she had ever discussed with any of the women she worked with.

She had been out with several boys of her own age up to the age of nineteen, but after her parents had died she had been too busy trying to keep a home for Toby and herself—hadn't really had much time to think about relationships. Which was probably the reason she had fallen for Gareth's charm six months ago!

But in the face of Patrick's sophistication, his obvious experience when it came to women, she must seem rather gauche and naïve.

Well, tough! She had no intention of pretending an experience she just didn't have. And that included appearing sophisticated in the face of Patrick's appreciative comments on her body!

'Coffee, Ellie,' he reminded her lightly, moving to sit down at the kitchen table.

'Of course.' She moved economically about the kitchen, getting out the cups, cream and sugar, all the time avoiding Patrick's gaze, but knowing it followed her every movement.

'Did Davies—? Steady,' Patrick soothed as a spoon

landed on the floor with a clatter when Ellie just dropped it.

She bent to pick it up, her face averted so that he shouldn't see the heated colour in her cheeks.

'Ellie?'

Just that. Her name. Nothing else. But it was said compellingly enough for Ellie to know he wanted her to look across at him. And she did exactly that. The steadiness of his gaze as he looked at her wordlessly was as forceful as Ellie had known it would be.

'What do you want to know, Patrick?' she snapped impatiently, picking up the tray of coffee things only to put it down noisily on the kitchen table. 'Whether Gareth and I came close to being lovers?' she bit out sarcastically. 'What business is it of yours if we did?' she added challengingly, blue eyes bright with anger as she glared down at him.

'Black, no sugar,' he told her economically. 'My preference for coffee,' he explained mildly at her blank look.

'Oh. Fine,' she muttered, sitting down abruptly to concentrate all her attention on pouring the coffee. She didn't want to think about anything else!

'You're quite right, Ellie,' Patrick began softly, 'it is none of my business just how—intimate your relationship was with Davies. Except...'

She looked up sharply. 'Yes?'

His gaze was intense on the paleness of her face. 'Did he hurt you, Ellie?'

She felt the blood drain completely from her cheeks, her hand shook as she held the coffee pot poised over one of the cups.

'Ellie?'

She drew in a deep breath, swallowed hard, willing herself to carry on pouring the coffee without spilling it. No, Gareth hadn't hurt her, he had humiliated her. But it wasn't an incident she particularly wanted to relate to Patrick. It was the reason she knew she had meant absolutely nothing to Gareth—the reason she knew what sort of man he really was...

She gave an over-bright smile, her gaze not quite meeting Patrick's as she handed him his cup of coffee. 'It isn't important, Patrick,' she dismissed lightly. 'We're all agreed that he isn't a nice person.'

Patrick reached out, his hand covering hers as it rested on the tabletop. 'Tell me what happened,' he encouraged huskily.

She closed her eyes, wishing she could shut out the memory of that last time she had been with Gareth but at the same time knowing that she couldn't.

Gareth called into her office as she was finishing work, suggesting that he drive her home. Things had been rather strained between them the last couple of weeks— forgotten telephone calls, cancelled dates—and she had welcomed this chance to talk to him alone for a while.

Toby was still at work when they arrived back at the house, and almost before Ellie and Gareth were in the door, it seemed, Gareth began to kiss her. But as the kiss deepened, with Gareth's hands roaming more freely over her body than ever before, Ellie began to pull away from him.

'Don't,' she told him frowningly, at the same time

pushing ineffectually at his painful hold about her waist.

He smiled then—a smile like no other Ellie had seen him give, a smile so scornful it made her cringe. 'That's always been the trouble with you, Ellie,' he told her scathingly as he released her so abruptly she staggered slightly. 'Maybe if you hadn't been so frigid I wouldn't have needed to find someone else. As it is...'

Ellie stared at him. She had suspected something; of course she had. Gareth had been far too elusive these last two weeks for her not to have realised that something had gone seriously wrong with their relationship.

Gareth raised blond brows at her stricken expression. 'Of course, it isn't too late,' he drawled suggestively. 'I could still be persuaded into continuing our relationship. If you were to—'

'You conceited—!' Ellie broke off angrily, glaring up at him disgustedly. 'Let me get this right, Gareth,' she said evenly, eyes narrowed now. 'If I'll agree to go to bed with you then you'll consider breaking off your other—relationship?'

The fact that he had another relationship had come as a complete shock to her. But she would think about that later. Once Gareth had left. Because he *was* leaving. Soon!

He smiled. 'Well, I wouldn't go quite that far,' he mocked.

Her eyes widened. 'You're suggesting that I become part of some harem?'

'Of course not, Ellie.' He chuckled. 'If everything goes according to plan, I should be getting married soon. But that's no reason for us to break off our relationship. If things were different between us,' he added pointedly.

If everything went according to plan! What plan?

She swallowed hard. 'If the two of us were lovers, you mean?' she clarified icily.

Gareth shrugged. 'Well, it would hardly be worth the risk otherwise, now, would it?'

'Get out,' Ellie told him shakily, her hand on the table beside her for support; her legs felt so shaky she thought she might fall over otherwise.

'Now, Ellie, there's no reason to be like that,' he cajoled huskily, taking a step towards her.

She straightened, her chin raised challengingly. 'I said, get out, Gareth, and I meant it. And God help the poor woman you're planning to marry,' she added disgustedly.

He had come to a halt some distance away from her. 'Frigid,' he repeated scornfully.

Her eyes glazed coldly. 'You'll never know,' she bit out forcefully.

He smiled. 'But I already do know, Ellie,' he assured her derisively. 'Oh, well.' He shrugged in the face of her stony expression. 'I made the offer. See you around.' He raised a hand in farewell before letting himself out of the house.

She turned to Patrick now, having no intention of relating any of that conversation to him. It was bad enough that she still remembered every painfully humiliating word of it, without sharing it with anyone else. Least of all Patrick!

She gave him a dismissive smile. 'It isn't important

what happened, Patrick,' she told him lightly. 'Gareth hurt me with words, that's all. And as my mother always said, ''sticks and stones may break my bones, but words can never hurt me'',' she quoted ruefully.

Patrick looked unconvinced. 'Bones heal; words can never be forgotten.'

How true that was. She hadn't forgotten a single word Gareth had said to her six weeks ago, whereas a broken finger or wrist would have healed and been dismissed by now.

'Surely it's Gareth's problem if he considers that any woman who doesn't want to sleep with him must be frigid.' She shrugged.

Grey eyes widened. 'He actually said that? To *you*?' Patrick sounded incredulous.

Ellie gave him a disgruntled frown. 'Yes, he said that to me,' she repeated irritably.

Patrick chuckled softly. 'You're right, Ellie.' He gave a rueful shake of his head. 'He isn't important,' he explained at her questioning look. 'He obviously didn't get to know you very well at all, did he?' he added derisively.

'Exactly what do you mean by that remark?' she demanded defensively.

He looked at her consideringly before answering. 'Ellie, you are one of the warmest, most responsive women I have ever had the pleasure to meet.'

Her cheeks coloured hotly. It was no good denying what he said; her response to him whenever he touched her was undeniable.

'I'll tell you something else,' Patrick added huskily as he stood up to move round the table and pull her unresistingly to her feet. 'I'm glad Davies never got close enough to you to discover that for himself,' he murmured throatily, before bending to lightly brush Ellie's lips with his own.

So was she.

She hadn't always felt that way, had wondered in the days and then weeks that had followed Gareth's abrupt departure from her life whether she could indeed be frigid. But she only had to be in the same room with Patrick to be completely aware of him, and when she was actually in his arms like this…!

No, she wasn't frigid. She was just a woman who only responded to the right man. The right man for her. Because, although he was unsuitable in every other way—rich, powerful, successful, completely removed from her own lifestyle—she knew she had fallen in love with Patrick McGrath.

She had been fighting that knowledge for some time now, refusing to allow the thought to even enter her head. But alone here with him in the silence of her kitchen, held in his arms, their two bodies moulded perfectly together, she could no longer deny how she felt about him.

To herself, at least.

To Patrick it was another matter!

'Well, I'm relieved to hear it,' she told him lightly, at the same time moving determinedly out of his arms. 'Maybe there's hope for me after all,' she added with deliberate self-derision.

Patrick's gaze followed her frowningly. 'Ellie—'

'I just heard a car in the driveway, so I think Toby

must be home,' she told him with a certain amount of relief.

Her mother used to say something else to her, about 'jumping from the frying pan into the fire'. Well, she had certainly done that where Patrick was concerned; he was a more unsuitable man for her to have fallen in love with than Gareth had ever been!

CHAPTER EIGHT

'DID you enjoy yourself on Saturday?'

Ellie gave a startled glance towards the open door of her office, her gaze narrowing as she focused on Gareth standing in the doorway, looking incredibly cheerful. As well as self-confident.

The latter instantly made Ellie more wary than she would normally have been in his unwanted presence, and she glanced towards the door that connected hers to George's, to make sure it was firmly shut, before replying. 'The Delacortes gave you and Sarah a wonderful engagement party,' she answered non-committally.

Gareth grinned, coming fully into the room before closing the door behind him. 'That didn't exactly answer my question, now, did it?' he reproved derisively, moving to sit on the edge of her desk as he looked down at her with mocking blue eyes.

Ellie sighed. 'I didn't think it really needed an answer,' she dismissed, still eyeing him warily, sure his pleasantness wouldn't last for long; nowadays it usually didn't.

Besides, she remembered all too well his nastiness on Saturday evening. Still had the bruises to prove how angry he had been then.

He shrugged. 'Thanks for the cut-glass crystal vase, by the way. Sarah will be writing to everyone formally, of course, but I thought I would come and thank you personally.'

Cut-glass crystal vase? Ellie had been aware that Patrick had carried a gift-wrapped present into the house on Saturday evening, of course, but even if it had been a cut class crystal vase, what did it have to do with her...?

'''Congratulations, love from Patrick and Ellie'',' Gareth continued tauntingly. 'You've been ''Patrick and Ellie'' for how long?' he added scathingly.

A matter of days. Except they weren't 'Patrick and Ellie' at all.

She'd had no idea that Patrick had put her name beside his on the gift card that had accompanied the engagement present he'd given to his cousin on Saturday. She realised why he had done it, of course, but he might have warned her!

She gave Gareth a stony look. 'Gareth, I have no idea why you should be in the least interested,' she scorned.

'I'm not. Not really.' He still looked incredibly pleased with himself. 'It will be quite a coup for the Fairfax family if you and Toby manage to pull this off.' He gave her an admiring look. 'I must say, Ellie, you're something of a surprise. Especially after your holier-than-thou attitude before.' He shook his head. 'Those people in glass houses shouldn't throw stones, you know.'

Ellie gave him a suspicious look. Could he possibly have been drinking? Admittedly it was only eleven-thirty in the morning, but she couldn't think of any other explanation for the fact that what he was saying made absolutely no sense to her.

She shook her head, not wanting to prolong this unwanted conversation any further by asking him for an explanation. 'I'll bear your advice in mind, Gareth,' she dismissed. 'Now, if you wouldn't mind, I have some work to do…?' She gave a pointed look at where he sat on some of the papers on her desk.

Gareth grinned, making no effort to move. 'Don't you see, Ellie? There's no longer any need to be all coy with me. The truth is, you and I are more alike than I would ever have guessed.'

She stiffened defensively. 'I don't think so!' she snapped distastefully.

'But of course we are,' he contradicted happily. 'It's a pity you came on so prim and proper six weeks ago; you and I would have made a great team. And Toby, of course.'

He *had* been drinking; there was no other explanation for this completely puzzling conversation!

'What on earth does Toby have to do with any of this?' She looked at him impatiently.

The two men had met on several occasions, when Gareth had come to call for her at the house, but as far as she was aware Toby hadn't particularly taken to the other man then, and he certainly didn't like him now. As for Gareth, he hadn't seemed particularly interested in Toby either.

Gareth grinned. 'You can stop the pretence now, Ellie,' he teased. 'The game is up, so to speak. Maybe the three of us should form some sort of club? We could call it—'

'Gareth, I have no idea what you're talking about.' Ellie lost all patience with him. 'Besides which, you're sitting on my desk when I want to get on with some work. Now, would you please go?' She glared at him.

He stood up slowly. But looked no less confident. 'Okay, play it that way if you want to.' He shrugged. 'But just remember that if you keep my little secret then I'll keep yours. And Toby's, of course,' he added enigmatically. 'Fair's fair, after all.'

'Gareth—'

'Ellie, I'm just going across to—Gareth...?' George came to a halt in the doorway that connected his office to Ellie's, his gaze narrowing suspiciously on the younger man as he saw him standing there.

Gareth looked completely unconcerned by the interruption. 'I just popped in to tell Ellie how much Sarah and I loved the crystal vase she and Patrick gave us for an engagement present,' he told his future father-in-law lightly.

'Well, now you've told her might I suggest you leave her to get on with her work?' George nodded abruptly, continuing to look at the younger man with narrowed eyes.

'Of course,' Gareth accepted smoothly, moving unhurriedly to the door. 'I believe I'm seeing you and Mary for dinner this evening,' he added with a smile.

'I believe you are,' George acknowledged noncommittally.

'See you later, Ellie,' came Gareth's parting shot.

Not if she saw him first! She had found him obnoxious enough before. Now she not only disliked him intensely, she didn't understand a word he said!

George gave a shuddering sigh. 'No matter how hard

I try, I simply can't bring myself to like that young man.' He shook his head sadly.

Ellie gave a wan smile. 'I wouldn't worry about it, George; you're in the majority rather than the minority!'

He grimaced. 'I wouldn't worry about it at all if Sarah hadn't decided to marry the man! I had just about decided that he wasn't suitable for Delacorte, Delacorte and Delacorte when Sarah dropped the bombshell of her engagement to the man. Her mother and I simply don't know what to do for the best,' he added heavily.

Ellie gave him a sympathetic smile. 'I think the two of you are doing very well. Very often seeming to do nothing is the right thing to do,' she added encouragingly.

George gave her a grateful smile. 'A word of advice, Ellie. Never have daughters; it plays the very devil with your heart.'

She felt so sorry for him. Especially as there was nothing she could say or do to make him feel any better.

He straightened, seeming to shake off his despondency as he glanced down at the file he held in his hand. 'I'm just going across to Gerald's office for a few minutes. My next appointment is at twelve-thirty?'

Ellie nodded after a brief glimpse at the appointment book on her desk, breathing a sigh of relief when she was finally left alone in her office.

Gareth's conversation was still a complete puzzle to her. But then, the man himself was a complete enigma to her; how could he possibly be contemplating marrying someone he so obviously didn't love? As beautiful as Sarah was.

And how could she be in love with a man when she stood absolutely no chance of him ever feeling the same way about her?

Ellie had pondered that question several times over the weekend, and she still had no answer. Only knew that she was counting the hours until she saw Patrick again!

'Oh, good, you got the message and aren't dressed up,' Patrick said with relief as Ellie opened the door to him at eight o'clock on Tuesday evening.

She raised dark brows. 'It would serve you right if I said that I was dressed up.' She opened the door wider to let him in, wearing a fitted blue jumper with faded denims.

He shook his head, grinning. 'I knew Toby wouldn't let me down!'

Her brother had dutifully passed on Patrick's message earlier that they were going to eat at a pizzeria, and Ellie had dressed accordingly. Although Patrick looked as ruggedly handsome as ever in the black sweater and black denims that he wore.

'We always seem to be going somewhere formal,' Patrick dismissed. 'I thought it would be nice if we could completely relax this evening.'

There was also no possibility of them running into anyone Patrick knew in some out-of-the-way pizzeria!

Ellie had had plenty of time to think once Toby had passed on Patrick's message to dress casually because they were going to eat informally. Patrick had never said, and she hadn't liked to ask Toby, but there was always the possibility that Patrick actually had a woman in his life at the moment. Perhaps not someone he had wanted to introduce to his family, as in accompanying him to the party on Saturday evening, but that didn't mean he wasn't involved in a relationship. She had never thought to ask…

But she wanted to ask now—wanted to know everything there was to know about Patrick McGrath. Especially if there was already a woman in his life!

Not that Ellie didn't already know she was wasting her time feeling about him as she did; she just didn't like the idea of Patrick having to explain these dates with her to another woman. In fact, she just didn't like the thought of there being another woman at all!

'I hope you like Italian food?' Patrick prompted ruefully.

'I like it fine.' Ellie nodded, picking up her fleecy blue jacket from the kitchen chair—if only to show him that she didn't always wear the unattractive long black coat.

The beautiful pashmina Patrick had bought for her on Saturday was now carefully folded and placed back in its tissue paper inside the box, stashed away at the back of her wardrobe. Ellie knew she might never find the opportunity to wear such a glamorous item again.

'Shall we go?' she prompted lightly once she had shrugged into the jacket.

Patrick looked at her consideringly. 'Is everything okay? Has Davies been bothering you again?' he added hardly.

Ellie frowned. 'Apart from a very strange conversation with him yesterday morning, no.'

'Tell me about it while we eat,' Patrick suggested,

opening the door for her. 'Unless you think it will give us both indigestion?' He grimaced as he moved to unlock the car door.

It was warm and cosy as she settled inside the car, which smelt vaguely of the aftershave Patrick favoured. 'No more than any other subject would, I don't suppose,' she answered Patrick dismissively as he got in beside her.

He gave her a sideways glance. 'What's that supposed to mean?'

Ellie sighed. 'I still don't know what this evening is about—'

Patrick shrugged. 'How about it's a thank-you for all the—inconvenience you're having to go through on my family's behalf?'

'What about the inconvenience you're now having to go to on my behalf?' she came back dismissively.

He frowned his puzzlement as he drove. 'What inconvenience would that be?'

She gave a self-derisive smile. 'Taking me out.'

He smiled ruefully. 'I have no idea what you're talking about, Ellie.'

She grimaced. 'It must be the week for it!'

'Forget Davies for the moment,' Patrick bit out impatiently. 'I want to know what you meant by that remark just now.'

Seeing the determination on his face, Ellie wished she had never made the remark in the first place. She was just feeling sorry for herself because she had fallen in love with a man who was completely unobtainable. Which was absolutely no reason to try and make life difficult for him on the rare occasions she saw him!

'Forget it,' she advised self-derisively. 'It's just pre-Christmas tension, I expect. It's very kind of you to take me out—'

'Ellie, I know you haven't known me very long,' he interrupted evenly, his expression grim, 'but when you do know me better you'll realise that, although I'm not a cruel man, neither am I someone who takes a woman out—namely you—because I am simply being kind!'

She had seen Patrick in many moods over the last couple of weeks—amused, attentive, charming, angry when it came to Gareth—but he had never been annoyed or angry with her before. At the moment he appeared to be both!

'I'm sorry if I've mistaken the situation—'

'And don't start apologising,' he cut in impatiently. 'You have done nothing to apologise for. I appear to be the one who hasn't made myself clear. A fact I am about to change right now,' he assured her determinedly, and he turned the car into a deserted private car park on the edge of town.

'What are you doing?' Ellie looked about them dazedly as Patrick parked the car in the middle of the dimly lit area.

He released his seat belt before turning in his seat to face her. 'I'm about to convince you that I asked you out this evening for one reason and one reason only. You can let me know afterwards if I've succeeded or not,' he added firmly, before reaching out to pull her into his arms, his mouth coming down forcefully on hers.

Ellie was so stunned by the suddenness of the kiss that for a moment she lay acquiescent in his arms, but then the magical thrill of his lips thoroughly exploring hers warmed her body in that familiar way, and her arms moved up about his shoulders as she returned the kiss with all the pent-up longing inside her.

Patrick's hands moved caressingly along the length of her spine, sending ripples of pleasure through her whole body. Her neck arched as his lips moved from her mouth to her cheek, and then down the creamy column of her throat, his tongue doing amazing things to the tiny hollow he discovered there.

Ellie's eyes were closed, her head back against the car seat, her fingers entwined the thick darkness of Patrick's hair as she held him against her.

'Are you wearing anything underneath this jumper, Ellie Fairfax?' Patrick murmured throatily as his thumb moved across the tip of one hardened nipple.

'What do you think, Patrick McGrath?' she came back huskily.

'I think perhaps I should find out,' he said softly.

Ellie gasped at the first touch of his hands on her nakedness. They were cool as they cupped the warmth of her breasts, the moistness of his tongue against the hardened tips causing her back to arch instinctively, and she moaned low in her throat at the pleasure that swept heatedly through her body.

She felt mindless, every bone in her body fluid as the warmth of Patrick's mouth closed erotically over one hardened nipple. Her own hands moved restlessly up and down the long length of his back as she wished the pleasure to go on for ever.

Patrick's hands encircled her waist as he held her against him, his lips travelling down the flat slope of her midriff now, pausing to explore the dip of her navel revealed by the low-waisted denims.

Even that felt wonderful, Ellie realised with a surprised gasp, leading her to wonder what other parts of her body would respond to Patrick's slightest touch.

Patrick raised his head to look at her, his eyes bright in the semi-darkness. 'I'm not hurting you?'

'Oh, no,' she breathed weakly, feeling as if she must have died and gone to heaven.

'And do you know now why I invited you out to dinner?' he prompted huskily.

'Er—yes, I think so.' She nodded; it was a little disconcerting looking at him over her bared breasts!

'You only *think* so?' he murmured teasingly, eyes glinting with intent. 'Perhaps I wasn't convincing enough—'

'Oh, yes—you were!' She reached down and raised his head as he would have commenced kissing her breasts again. 'Patrick—'

'I know.' He grimaced self-derisively as he gently pulled her jumper down to cover her nakedness. 'This isn't the ideal place for lovemaking. In fact—' he straightened, running his hand restlessly through hair already tousled by Ellie's own hands '—I think I'm a little old to be making love in a car park. But later, Ellie, when I get you home…!'

'Promises, promises,' she teased self-consciously.

'Be warned, Ellie,' he told her decisively, 'I always keep my promises.'

Had Patrick really just made love to her? Had he really just paid homage to her body as if he found her beautiful and desirable?

He most certainly had!

And, what was more, he'd said he was going to do it all over again once they returned from their evening out!

The rest of the evening—the Italian restaurant, the delicious food they ate there, the easy flow of conversation—all passed in a dream for Ellie.

She learnt that Patrick had gone to university, eventually leaving with a first class degree in Business Studies, and that instead of going into industry working for someone else had put his knowledge to use on a personal basis, building up a varied and successful business over the last fifteen years. It was a challenge he obviously still enjoyed.

She also learnt that his was a very close family, that his sister Teresa was fourteen years younger than his thirty-eight, also that she was the cherished baby of the family.

What Ellie still hadn't established by the time Patrick drove her home was whether or not he had a woman in his life; it didn't seem the sort of thing she should ask him after their intimacy earlier this evening!

'Damn,' he muttered as they arrived at Ellie's home and saw Toby's car was already parked in the driveway.

Ellie felt warmth in her cheeks as she guessed the reason for his irritation: Toby's presence meant that they wouldn't be able to carry on where they had left off earlier after all.

Patrick turned to look at her ruefully after parking the car behind Toby's. 'Have you never thought of getting a home of your own?' he said dryly.

Until this moment, quite honestly, no. It had always

seemed the natural thing for her and Toby to continue living together after their parents' death. But at this moment Ellie had to admit she was disappointed that they weren't to be alone again, too.

'Never mind.' She squeezed Patrick's arm lightly. 'It can't be helped,' she added ruefully.

'You're right. There will be other occasions.' He nodded before getting agilely out of the car to come round and open her door for her.

Ellie felt as if she were floating on air as they walked over to the house; Patrick had said there would be other occasions. That must mean he was going to ask to see her again.

To her surprise, Toby was nowhere to be found once they were inside the house.

'He must have gone to bed.' Ellie shrugged dismissively.

Patrick moved so that he was standing very close to her. 'Does that mean we're alone after all?'

'I suppose it must do. I—' Ellie broke off as she heard the sound of feet descending the stairs. 'Perhaps not,' she added ruefully, turning expectantly towards the doorway that led out into the hallway.

Except it wasn't Toby who came into the kitchen!

But Ellie had no trouble placing the other woman as the one who had looked so interestedly at Toby at the party on Saturday evening. And if she had been upstairs with Toby...!

'Thank goodness you're here,' the other woman burst out agitatedly.

Although it wasn't to Ellie that she spoke...

'What is it?' Patrick was instantly alert and left

Ellie's side to go to the other woman, the languid intimacy that had existed between the two of them all evening instantly broken.

'Toby,' the woman choked emotionally. 'I think it must be something he's eaten—I had to drive him here. He felt too ill even to drive home.' She looked distraught. 'Oh, Patrick, I'm so worried about him!' She launched herself into Patrick's arms, the tears starting to fall down her creamy cheeks.

Ellie looked at the two of them in total stupefaction. The other woman appeared to have spent the evening with Toby, and yet she and Patrick obviously knew each other rather well too. Of course, this woman had been at the party on Saturday evening, so the two might be related. Even so...

But for the moment she was too concerned about Toby herself to try to puzzle this one out, turning wordlessly to hurriedly leave the room and run upstairs to her brother's bedroom.

Toby looked awful. He lay weakly back against the pillows, his face waxen, his eyes dull with discomfort and pain as he looked up at Ellie.

'I'm going to call the doctor,' she told him decisively.

'Fine,' he nodded. 'Tell him to bring something with him to put me out of my misery!' he called after her as she hurried from the room.

Ellie turned to give a strained smile at his attempt to joke. At least, she hoped he was joking! 'I'll tell him.' She nodded before running down the stairs again. The fact that her brother hadn't argued about her calling in the doctor told her just how ill he must feel; Toby, like most men, absolutely hated the necessity of ever seeing a doctor.

'Food poisoning, do you think?' Patrick prompted economically as he came out into the hallway where she stood telephoning.

'I think so.' She nodded, frowning as she waited for her call to be answered. 'I—perhaps you could make some coffee for all of us?' she suggested distractedly.

'Teresa is already doing that,' he informed her grimly. 'Who are you calling?' he added frowningly.

Ellie stared him speechlessly. Teresa? The young woman who was at this very moment making coffee in the kitchen, the woman Toby had obviously spent the evening with, was Patrick's young *sister*, Teresa?

What—?

'Ellie, who are you telephoning?' Patrick repeated firmly.

'The doctor—' She broke off as Patrick shook his head grimly.

'I'll ring my own doctor and get him to come out.' He took the receiver from her hand, disconnecting her call and putting through one of his own.

Ellie could only stand by dazedly as Patrick spoke decisively with whoever had answered his call, not *asking* the doctor to come out and see Toby, but giving him the directions to do so.

The young woman in the kitchen—the same woman who had looked so interestedly at Toby on Saturday evening—was Patrick's sister, Teresa. Teresa? Tess...? That was a shortened version of the name Teresa, wasn't it? Could Patrick's sister possibly be the Tess that Toby had told Ellie he'd been dating the last couple of months?

And, if she was, why hadn't Toby ever told her that it was Patrick's sister he was dating?

Why hadn't Patrick told her?

Because she was absolutely positive, from the fact that Patrick hadn't looked in the least surprised to see his sister here, that he had known about the relationship before this evening!

What did it all mean?

CHAPTER NINE

'WOULD you like one or both of us to stay with you for the rest of the night?' Patrick asked Ellie some time later. The doctor had been to see Toby, and diagnosed—as they had all suspected he might—that her brother had food poisoning.

It had been an extremely traumatic couple of hours for Ellie, worried about Toby and completely puzzled by his relationship with Teresa/Tess.

But the idea of either Patrick or his sister staying for the rest of the night did not appeal to her. It also wasn't necessary. The doctor had given Toby an injection to stop him vomiting, and although her brother was still pale, he was now fast asleep.

'That won't be necessary,' Ellie answered Patrick distantly. None of the tension she had felt earlier, at discovering Toby's girlfriend Tess was in fact Patrick's sister Teresa, had evaporated.

In fact, if anything it was worse, all sorts of suspicions and conclusions having popped into Ellie's head over the last couple of hours. Most of them too depressing to contemplate for long!

'I'm very grateful for your help in getting a doctor here so promptly,' she added as she realised she probably sounded less than polite.

'But now you want us to leave?' Patrick guessed ruefully.

It was almost one o'clock in the morning. She was incredibly weary from the worry over Toby, and her head ached from the circles her thoughts were going round and round in. So, yes, she wanted him—and his sister—to leave now.

She glanced at the younger woman, Teresa, sitting dejectedly at the kitchen table staring into a cup of cold coffee, her face pale.

Ellie could see a faint family resemblance between the brother and sister now—both were dark, with those magnetic grey eyes—but where Patrick's face was all ruggedly sharp angles Teresa's was softened into gamine beauty.

Why hadn't she seen that resemblance on Saturday evening?

Because she hadn't been looking for it! Because no one had told her that Toby's girlfriend Tess *was* Patrick's young sister!

That was what really bothered Ellie about all this; why had no one told her of the relationship?

Until she had the answer to that, she felt the more distance she put between Patrick and herself the better.

'If you don't mind,' she answered Patrick evenly. 'I wouldn't expect Toby in to work tomorrow either, if I were you,' she added dryly; she doubted her brother would be strong enough to get out of bed in the morning, let alone anything else!

'I wasn't,' Patrick dismissed impatiently, looking down at her frowningly. 'Ellie—'

'Patrick, I don't think now is either the right time or place for the two of us to talk,' she bit out abruptly, moving sharply away from him, at the same time giving a pointed look in the direction of his sister.

Not that Teresa looked as if she were taking any notice of their conversation. She was completely wrapped up in the misery of her worry over Toby. Which probably meant that the affection Toby obviously felt for 'Tess' was reciprocated.

Why had no one told her that Toby was dating Patrick's sister?

But perhaps someone had, Ellie realised slowly, as she recalled Gareth's enigmatic conversation of yesterday...

Gareth had seemed to be under the impression that Toby, as well as herself, was no better than he was. Because he believed them both to be dating the McGrath brother and sister for the same reasons he had become engaged to Sarah—wealth and ambition? He was totally wrong, of course—on both counts. But—

'Ellie?'

She looked up to find Patrick watching her concernedly. 'Perhaps you should take your sister home now,' she suggested stiffly. 'She looks as if she's had enough for one evening,' she added, with a rueful glance at the younger woman.

'I think we all have.' Patrick nodded grimly. 'I'll call in tomorrow and see how Toby is.'

And continue this conversation, his words seemed to imply. Well, Ellie needed time and space to form her tangled thoughts into some sort of order. She wasn't sure twelve hours was long enough for that!

'Of course,' she accepted smoothly. 'Now, it really is late...'

He gave her another searching look before turning abruptly to his sister. 'It's time to go, Teresa,' he told her briskly. 'I'm sure Ellie will call us if she needs us,' he added as Teresa looked about to protest.

Considering the only telephone number she had for Patrick was his business one, that wouldn't really do a lot of good. Although Toby would have Patrick's mobile number.

'Of course I will,' Ellie assured the younger woman as Teresa gave her a distressed look.

Teresa stood up, very tall and slender. 'I'm really sorry we've had to meet for the first time under these circumstances.' She grimaced.

Yes, it might have been better—it definitely *would* have been better for Ellie!—if the two of them had met before now.

'I don't suppose Toby will feel like this for long, and then perhaps he can bring you here for a drink one evening,' she consoled.

Once he had given Ellie an explanation as to exactly what was going on! Because something *was* going on— Ellie was just too tired at this moment to be able to make sense of it all.

'Maybe the four of us could go out to dinner together at the weekend,' Patrick put in smoothly.

Ellie turned to give him a cool look. 'I think it would be better if we took one step at a time. Besides,' she added firmly as she saw Patrick was about to argue the point, 'I doubt Toby will feel up to eating anything for several days.' It was a valid point—one she could see Patrick would have a problem arguing with.

Thank goodness. She didn't want to tie herself down

to a definite time for seeing Patrick again. Not until she had some answers to a few pertinent questions. Answers that only her brother could give her.

'I'll ring you in the morning, if that's okay,' Teresa McGrath told her a few minutes later as she stood in the doorway preparing to leave.

'Of course,' Ellie accepted, deliberately avoiding looking at Patrick as he stood at his sister's side. 'Brr, it's cold out here.' She shivered from the icy wind blowing around them.

'Yes, it does seem to have turned a little icy,' Patrick murmured softly.

Ellie looked at him sharply as she sensed his double meaning, and those raised dark brows told her she hadn't been mistaken. 'The forecast is for snow,' she returned, deliberately meeting his gaze.

'Luckily it never settles for long in our climate,' he came back, just as deliberately.

Ellie shrugged. 'The forecast is for a long-term cold front.' Two could play at this game. And, until she knew exactly what was going on, a cold front was exactly what she intended showing Patrick McGrath.

He shrugged broad shoulders. 'Ice and snow eventually melt.'

'Eventually,' she echoed evenly.

'Patrick, you can discuss the weather another time; we really should go, and let Ellie get back inside out of this biting wind,' Teresa prompted her brother, obviously having no idea of the double-edged conversation that had been taking place between her brother and Ellie.

To Ellie they had sounded like a couple of secret

agents in a B-rated movie, talking in a code only the two of them understood!

'So we should.' Patrick nodded abruptly before bending his head and lightly brushing Ellie's mouth with his own. 'But I will be back in the morning, Ellie.'

A threat if ever she had heard one, Ellie decided irritably. Well, if, as the doctor had implied, Toby was better by the morning, Patrick would arrive here to find Toby recovering on his own and Ellie at work!

But not before she had spoken to Toby herself...

'I have no idea what you're talking about, sis.' Toby shook his head, his face still very pale as he lay back on the pillows. He had slept well through what had been left of the night, and the nausea seemed to have completely abated, although he had been left with a severe headache.

Join the club, Ellie thought, and gave a deep sigh before sitting on the side of her brother's bed. 'Okay, let's start this off simply: why did you omit to tell me that the Tess you have been dating the last few months is actually Teresa McGrath, Patrick's young sister?'

'I—'

'Please, don't tell me that you didn't think it was important,' Ellie advised him dryly—she sensed he was about to tell her exactly that. 'Because you know very well that it is. That it always was. That it still is,' she concluded pointedly.

'I'm not sure you should be badgering a sick man in this overly strident way.' Toby shook his head before lying back to close his eyes, having just risked consuming a cup of weak tea and a dry piece of toast, both of which seemed—so far—to have stayed down.

'It could get worse, Toby,' she warned him. 'If what I suspect is true, I could actually end up strangling this "sick man"—and so put *everyone* out of their misery!' Her eyes glittered dangerously.

She had had plenty of time to think during a rather sleepless night—and some of the conclusions she had come to had been less than reassuring!

Toby opened one eye to look at her with obvious reluctance. 'Why don't you tell me what you suspect—and then I'll tell you if it's right or not?'

'There's little point in doing that if you aren't going to answer me honestly!' she bit out sharply.

Both Toby's eyes opened innocently wide now. 'My big sister taught me to always tell the truth.'

'Very funny!' Ellie gave a humourless smile, getting up from the side of the bed to move impatiently about the room, her narrowed gaze fixed on her brother the whole time she did so. Finally she gave a heavy sigh. 'Are you and Teresa McGrath serious about each other?'

'Yes,' Toby answered unhesitatingly.

Ellie nodded; it was the answer she had expected. 'Why did Patrick McGrath agree to take me to the company Christmas dinner?'

Her brother frowned his puzzlement at this sudden change of subject. 'I told you—'

'I know what you told me, Toby,' she cut in impatiently. 'But now I want the real reason.'

He shook his head, wincing as it obviously caused him a certain amount of discomfort. 'But that *was* the real reason. Wasn't it?' he added uncertainly as Ellie looked unconvinced.

To Ellie's relief, her brother's answer told her one thing at least; whatever Patrick McGrath had been up to this last couple of weeks, Toby had obviously played no part in it. Which meant it had all been Patrick McGrath's own doing!

She had thought about several of the puzzling remarks Patrick had made this last week, about how much Toby cared for her, how her young brother felt a responsibility towards her, and all those questions about why she didn't have someone else in her life after Gareth—questions that all seemed to lead to the same unpleasant conclusion.

She was even more convinced about it now she knew from Toby that his relationship with Teresa McGrath was a serious one: Patrick was desperately trying to clear the way—clear Ellie out of the way, if only temporarily—in order to secure his young sister's happiness with Toby.

'Toby, why didn't you just tell me about Tess?' she prompted gently.

'But I did tell you about her,' he answered evasively.

Ellie shook her head. 'Only when the two of you were going out. Nothing else about her. Certainly not that the two of you are in love with each other. Why was that?'

Toby drew in a ragged breath. 'I'm sure that was just what you wanted to hear two months ago!' he bit out disgustedly.

Two months ago? When she had suspected that Gareth was seeing someone else behind her back—six weeks ago when she had finally found out the truth and stopped seeing him?

'Oh, Toby!' she cried emotionally, tears misting her eyes now. 'I would be pleased to hear of your happiness at any time. Any time at all!' she repeated with affectionate exasperation.

Instead of which Toby had kept the seriousness of his relationship with Tess a secret in an effort not to hurt Ellie.

Patrick McGrath, it seemed, was the one who had taken it a step further than that!

She sat back on the side of the bed, taking her brother's hand in her own. 'Are you and Tess going to get married?'

Toby gave a start at the directness of the question, his gaze not quite meeting Ellie's searching one. 'Maybe—in time,' he answered evasively.

It was just as she had thought!

Toby and Tess *were* serious about each other, and until six weeks ago it must have looked as if Ellie was in a serious relationship too. But that had all come crashing down around her ears, leaving Toby feeling the responsibility towards her that Patrick had mentioned.

She could see exactly what had happened now— knew that Toby, despite numerous protestations on her part, felt he owed her an emotional debt for taking care of him after their parents died. The fact that her relationship with Gareth had fallen apart under unpleasant circumstances had triggered Toby into putting his own relationship with Teresa McGrath on hold.

Except Patrick obviously had other ideas where his sister's happiness was concerned...

So much for what Ellie had thought—hoped—was developing between the two of them!

'No ''maybe'', Toby,' she told her brother firmly now, standing up. 'No ''in time'' either,' she added decisively. 'If you love the girl, and she loves you, then you should ask her to marry you.'

Toby grimaced sheepishly. 'I already have.'

'When?' Ellie prompted sharply.

'Eight weeks ago,' he admitted reluctantly.

Ellie raised dark brows. 'And?'

The grimace turned to a self-conscious smile. 'She said yes.'

Ellie gave an emotional laugh. 'You are an idiot, Toby,' she told him affectionately. 'You've asked her; she's said yes. The next move is to buy her a ring. Then arrange the wedding. I'll be there to dance at it,' she promised. 'Am I making myself clear, Toby?' she teased.

He grinned widely. 'Very.'

'Good.' She nodded her satisfaction. 'I'll just have to learn to cope with having the arrogant Patrick McGrath as some sort of relative.' She frowned.

Toby frowned too. 'But I thought you liked him?'

Too much!

She swallowed hard, straightening determinedly; after all, there was such a thing as pride involved here—her own! 'He's your boss, Toby; of course I had to be pleasant to him. Now that he's going to be your brother-in-law too, I'll just have to continue being pleasant to him. It shouldn't be that difficult; with any luck I'll see very little of him,' she dismissed scathingly, turning to leave the bedroom—and finding herself face to face with a stricken Teresa McGrath!

Ellie looked at the other woman searchingly, knowing by her unhappy expression that she had heard every word of Ellie's last statement...

CHAPTER TEN

'I KNOW I said I was going to telephone, but— I did knock on the kitchen door when I arrived, and when no one answered I let myself in,' Teresa explained awkwardly. 'I hope you don't mind?' she added with a self-conscious grimace.

Mind? Of course Ellie didn't mind the younger woman letting herself in—it was the remarks that Teresa had overheard her making about her brother that Ellie minded! It was one thing to say those things about Patrick to Toby—completely out of defence for her heart—quite another for a member of the McGrath family to have actually heard her saying them...

'Tess...?' Toby called hopefully from inside the bedroom.

Teresa's face visibly brightened. 'He's feeling better?'

'Much,' Ellie assured her warmly. 'I'll go down and make some coffee and leave the two of you to have a chat.' And, hopefully, regain some of her lost composure!

What she really wanted to happen was for the ground to open and swallow her up!

Ellie was shaking by the time she reached the sanctuary of the kitchen, sitting down weakly in one of the kitchen chairs before burying her face in her hands with a groan of self-disgust.

All she had wanted to do with those remarks she'd made to Toby was regain some of her damaged pride—and what she had succeeded in doing was probably alienating her future sister-in-law!

How could she explain that to Teresa without giving away the fact that she had fallen completely in love with Patrick?

Her groan of self-disgust turned to one of pain. She had fallen in love with Patrick, and all he had been doing was keeping her romantically occupied long enough to ensure that Toby announced his engagement to Teresa.

She was sure now that was all Patrick had been doing this last week or so. She was the one who had been stupid enough to take his attention seriously. To fall in love with him!

How to extricate herself without Patrick ever being aware of that fact, without completely losing her self-respect? That was the problem!

Out of the frying pan into the fire, once again sprang to mind.

She had thought her infatuation with the fickle Gareth was the worst thing she had ever done in her life, but falling in love with Patrick had to be so much worse. Because he wasn't fickle. The love she felt for him wouldn't be as easily shrugged off as her feelings for Gareth had been.

It was because she truly loved Patrick that she was now able to see her previous feelings for Gareth for exactly what they were!

But this time she would come out of it with at least

her pride intact, Ellie decided as she straightened determinedly. She had to!

The coffee was fresh in the pot, and cups, cream and sugar placed on the kitchen table by the time Teresa came downstairs ten minutes later. The smile on Ellie's face was warm and friendly.

'He's much better, isn't he?' she told Teresa lightly.

'Much.' The younger woman nodded, her expression slightly reserved.

Was that so surprising, when minutes ago Teresa had walked in on a conversation where Ellie had been totally dismissing any need for her to like this woman's brother?

Ellie drew in a ragged breath, deciding it was probably better to jump in at the deep end. 'Look, concerning what you overheard me saying about Patrick earlier—'

'Please,' Teresa cut in with an awkward wave of her hand. 'I know how—how Patrick can be sometimes. He really doesn't mean anything by it. He's just—well, he's used to being in charge.' She grimaced. 'Not that he's in the least arrogant about it.' She hastened to defend her brother. 'Usually he just charms people into submission!'

Ellie knew just how true that was!

She shook her head. 'That was still no reason for me to—to—Well, I'm sorry you overheard my remarks,' she concluded heavily.

Great, Ellie, she instantly chided herself. That was really apologising for being so rude earlier about Teresa's brother!

'Would you like some coffee?' she offered briskly.

Teresa turned to look at the things laid out on the kitchen table before glancing back at Ellie. 'That would be lovely, thank you.' She smiled before sitting down.

Somehow Ellie very much doubted this young woman was any more used to sitting down in a kitchen drinking coffee than Patrick was; it would most likely be served to them in the drawing room, by staff as efficient as George's had been on Saturday evening.

Which posed the disheartening thought: where did Toby fit into all this?

No doubt he and Teresa were in love—that was only too easy to see after last night!—but how would the two of them fare being married to each other when their backgrounds were so different? Toby, as Patrick's assistant, earned a very good wage, but he certainly couldn't keep Teresa in the life to which she was accustomed...

'I'm an interior designer.'

Ellie looked up from pouring the coffee to find Teresa McGrath smiling at her ruefully.

Had her thoughts been so obvious? Or was it just that Teresa had the same ability as Patrick to be able to read her thoughts in particular? After Ellie's earlier remarks about Patrick, that was a disquieting thought.

Ellie shook her head. 'I didn't mean—'

'I know.' The other woman reached out to give Ellie's hand a reassuring squeeze, giving a shake of her head as she chuckled huskily. 'It's only that I've already had all those particular conversations with Toby,' she admitted affectionately. 'He has this terrible dread that people will think he's only interested in me for my money.'

In the same way that Gareth was interested in Sarah!

'I know that he isn't,' Ellie said firmly.

'Of course he isn't.' Teresa's chuckle deepened. 'If you only knew the trouble I had getting Toby to go out with me in the first place…!' She gave a shake of her head, dark hair silky on her shoulders. 'He seemed to think that as Patrick's sister I came under the heading of "untouchable."'

Ellie could well imagine that he had. In the same way she thought that Patrick was unobtainable to her…

'But you obviously managed to charm him into submission?' Ellie returned lightly.

'Not exactly.' Teresa smiled wistfully. 'I told Patrick how I felt about Toby, and he—well, he arranged for me to be around rather a lot—redesigning the offices he has here, and some new ones he's acquired in York.'

York…? Hadn't Patrick said something the other day about Toby being in York with another of his employees? Employee, indeed; his younger sister hardly came under that heading! And, no matter what Teresa might say to the contrary, the role of matchmaker that Patrick had adopted for himself was arrogance personified!

'I see.' Ellie nodded.

'Ellie—may I call you, Ellie?' Teresa paused politely.

'Of course,' she instantly acknowledged.

'Tess,' the other woman invited lightly. 'The family always calls me Teresa, but I prefer friends to call me Tess. And I do hope the two of us are going to be friends, Ellie…?'

For Toby's sake they would have to be. Although Ellie had to admit the McGrath family were very difficult to dislike, having a warm charm that drew like a magnet.

'Of course,' Ellie said again, wondering exactly where this conversation was leading.

Tess nodded, her expression intent now. 'I'm really not some little-rich-girl who saw something she wanted and instantly had her wish granted by an over-indulgent older brother. I love Toby very much, and those differences between us that you were thinking of earlier are totally unimportant.'

'Now,' Ellie felt compelled to point out.

Tess gave a definite shake of her head. 'Ever. Yes, my parents are rich. Yes, my brother is successful, and also rich. But we were both brought up with the belief that we had to make our own way in the world, to earn our own living. We were never going to just sit around waiting to inherit. I know how awful that sounds—' Tess grimaced as Ellie gave a surprised choking noise '—but it's exactly the way a lot of children of wealthy parents behave nowadays.'

'I wouldn't know.' Ellie laughed incredulously.

Once again Tess reached out and squeezed her hand. 'You don't need to—the closeness you and Toby have makes you so much richer than a wealth of money could ever do. I hope you will allow me to become part of that closeness…?' She gave Ellie a wistful look.

How could she resist this charming young woman? How could Toby have resisted her? Obviously he couldn't!

And if Toby and Tess's marriage meant that she would have to see more of Patrick than was comfortable, then she would have to learn to live with that.

Because she had no intention of taking anything away from the love Tess and Toby had found together.

Ellie gave the other woman a warm smile. 'I can't wait to dance at your wedding,' she assured her—and instantly wished she hadn't. That was exactly the remark she had made earlier—before coming out with her insulting remark about Patrick!

A remark Tess remembered all too well if her teasing smile was anything to go by. 'So you said.' She nodded.

Ellie felt the colour warm her cheeks. 'I really wish you hadn't overheard those remarks.' She grimaced.

Tess chuckled, grey eyes warm with humour. 'I wouldn't worry about it, Ellie; I'm sure Patrick has had much worse said to his face!'

'But not from his future—I'm not quite sure what the relationship is between the brother and sister of the bride and groom!' Ellie frowned.

'Neither am I.' Tess grinned. 'But, as I said, don't worry about it; if need be, Patrick is perfectly capable of standing up for himself.'

'And *do* I need to?'

Ellie swung round guiltily at the sound of Patrick's voice behind her, the colour in her cheeks fiery-red now as she saw the narrow-eyed way he was looking at her.

'I heard the two of you talking and decided not to disturb you by knocking on the door.' He shrugged, coming fully into the kitchen to close the door behind him.

Not to disturb her! Patrick disturbed Ellie every time she so much as looked at him! Did no one in this family ever knock?

She stood up abruptly. 'We were just having a cup of coffee. Would you like one?' she invited awkwardly.

'No, thanks,' he dismissed. 'What I would really like—'

'Toby is much better today,' Tess cut in brightly. 'He was asleep earlier, but I'm sure he will want to see you.' She stood up, a slight figure in fitted denims and a thick black sweater.

Patrick's gaze hadn't wavered from Ellie's stricken face. 'You go up; I'll join you in a moment,' he told his sister slowly.

'Oh, but—'

'I'll come upstairs once I've spoken to Ellie,' Patrick told Tess firmly.

Tess gave Ellie a sympathetic glance before leaving the kitchen, both women knowing that when Patrick spoke in that tone of voice there was no point in arguing with him.

The very air seemed to crackle with tension once Ellie and Patrick had been left alone in the kitchen. Ellie busied herself clearing the used cups from the table to put them in the dishwasher. At least that way she didn't have to look at Patrick!

But she was very aware of him standing behind her, of every magnetic inch of him, his dark hair, that aristocratic face, the business suit, white shirt and grey tie that in no way detracted from the powerful body beneath.

Was it always going to be like this? Ellie wondered in dismay. Would she still feel this complete awareness of him, this love for him, in all the years to come?

Years when he would probably marry and have children of his own? She hoped not!

'What's going on, Ellie?'

She drew in a controlling breath before turning to face him, a brightly meaningless smile curving her lips. 'I have no idea what you mean.' She kept her tone deliberately light. 'I like Tess, by the way,' she added—before he could tell her exactly what he had meant by that earlier remark! 'I'm sure she and Toby are going to be very happy together.'

'No doubt.' He nodded uninterestedly, eyes still narrowed as he looked at her searchingly. 'Look, I'm sorry you had to find out about the two of them in the way that you did—'

'Don't be silly, Patrick,' she said derisively. 'In fact, I have no idea what the big secret was in the first place,' she continued hardly, her head back challengingly. 'Toby is twenty-six and I'm twenty-seven; it's well past time one of us moved on.'

She couldn't pretend—to herself, at least—that it wouldn't be a little strange, no longer having Toby's less than peaceful presence around the house—that she wouldn't miss the way he never shut a door behind him, left the bathroom in a shocking mess every morning and more often than not forgot to put his washing in the wash-basket, but she had never been under any illusion that the status quo would continue indefinitely. Her brother was a handsome young man, for goodness' sake; Ellie had never doubted that he would eventually find someone he loved and wanted to marry.

The fact that the woman Toby loved was the sister of the man Ellie had been stupid enough to fall in love with herself was just something she would have to learn to live with!

'Ellie—'

'Patrick,' she cut in firmly, blue eyes flashing a warning now. 'I'm aware that you've been acting as—as some sort of ambassador for Toby and Tess this last ten days or so, but there really was no need!'

Patrick's mouth tightened now, a nerve pulsing in his jaw. 'Is that really what you think has been happening this last week?'

'Of course,' she dismissed scathingly, desperately hoping that none of the aching love she felt for him showed in her face or eyes. 'Not that I don't appreciate the fact that you came to the company dinner with me. It's nice to finally know that it was actually an attempt on your part to further family relations.'

Patrick took a step towards her. 'You think that's the only reason I agreed to accompany you to that dinner?' he murmured huskily.

Ellie stood her ground, even though every particle of her cried out for her to move away from her complete physical awareness of him. 'Of course,' she said again. 'Oh, I'm aware there was also a curiosity on your part to meet your cousin's fiancée on neutral territory, but other than that—' she shrugged '—it must have been quite a chore for you.'

His eyes suddenly glittered silver. 'Exactly what is going on, Ellie?' he rasped. 'Last night—'

She gave a dismissive laugh. 'Last night I think the two of us may have got a little carried away by the roles we've been playing—'

'Last night I didn't think we were playing any roles. I thought we went out to dinner together for no other reason than I asked you and you accepted!' Patrick insisted harshly.

And she shouldn't have done! Shouldn't ever have allowed herself the luxury of believing there was any future in a relationship between Patrick and herself. In fact, now that she was aware of the reason behind Patrick's attentions, she knew very well that there wasn't a future in it!

She forced another rueful laugh. 'Then you thought wrong,' she bit out derisively.

He took another step towards her, so close now Ellie could feel the heat of his body against her sensitised skin. 'I didn't imagine your response to me last night.' He spoke gruffly now.

'Or your own to me,' she came back, with a defensive arch of her brows. 'I'm not denying there's an attraction between us—it would be silly to even try. As I said, I think we both got a little carried away with the moment. But it really wouldn't do—in the circumstances,' she continued, determined though Patrick would have interrupted once again, 'for the two of us to indulge in a meaningless affair.'

Patrick's mouth tightened. 'Meaningless...?' he repeated softly. Dangerously, to Ellie's ears.

But what did he expect from her? What did he want from her? She had already had one disastrous relationship this last year—and a relationship with Patrick promised to be even more catastrophic than that had turned out to be!

She shook her head. 'Patrick, I think, for Tess and Toby's sake, that we shouldn't pursue this attraction. After all,' she continued brightly, 'once the two of them are married, the two of us will be related too. Which could prove a little embarrassing if we've been silly enough to indulge in an affair.'

Patrick looked down at her searchingly, the silver gaze seeming to see deep into her soul.

Ellie stood that probing gaze for as long as she could—precisely thirty seconds!—before giving a lightly dismissive laugh. 'Patrick, isn't it already bad enough that I find going to work extremely uncomfortable, in case I have to see or speak to Gareth, without having that same discomfort concerning any necessity to see Toby's future in-laws?' She arched dark brows at him.

'You do care for him after all? Is that it?' Patrick rasped.

Care for Gareth? Absolutely not. Ellie could see him for exactly what he was now—and the knowledge was extremely unpleasant. As well as embarrassing.

But wasn't Patrick's suggestion giving her the perfect let-out for what promised to be an even more unacceptable situation…?

'I'm not sure what I feel any more.' She shrugged, though actually claiming to feel anything but contempt for Gareth was lodging in her throat and staying there. 'About anything,' she added firmly.

'I see.' Patrick's expression became unreadable and he moved away from her.

Did he? Somehow Ellie doubted that very much. But it was better this way, she told herself firmly. For all of them.

Except…the thought of not knowing when she would see Patrick again gave her a feeling of heaviness in her chest. She rushed into awkward speech 'Of course, I understand there's still a problem concerning Sarah's engagement to Gareth. And if there's anything more I can do to help—'

'Like winning Davies back yourself, for example?' Patrick rasped scathingly.

Ellie drew in a sharp breath at what she guessed was a deliberate insult. 'Somehow I don't think so,' she came back evenly; if she lost her temper she might just say things she would be better keeping to herself! Totally damning things, like how could she even *think* of looking at another man when she was desperately in love with Patrick?

'Then I think we've probably imposed on your good nature enough already,' Patrick assured her distantly, every haughty inch the successful businessman he was.

That heaviness in Ellie's chest instantly got heavier. Well, she had wanted to distance herself from this man, to keep her pride intact, and it appeared she had succeeded. Only too well!

But there was nothing more she could say or do now, without backing down from the stand she had made concerning any sort of a relationship between Patrick and herself.

She glanced at her wristwatch. 'If you'll excuse me? I really have to be going now. Toby is so much better, and I promised George I would try to get into the office before lunch,' she explained briskly.

Patrick nodded tersely. 'Teresa will probably want to stay with Toby for most of the day anyway.'

'Of course,' she accepted evenly, reluctant to go even after claiming that she had to. Reluctant to part from Patrick not knowing when she would see him again.

Oh, she knew she would see him again some time, at Toby and Tess's engagement and at their wedding, but they would be occasions crowded with lots of other people, when Patrick wouldn't even need to speak to her if he didn't want to. And after today she accepted he probably wouldn't want to.

Patrick gave her another searching glance before nodding abruptly. 'I'll go up and see Toby now.'

'Yes.' Ellie looked up at him, hoping all the aching longing she felt in her heart for him to hold her, to kiss her, wasn't evident in her eyes.

'I'll say goodbye, then.' He turned sharply on his heels and left the room, his back stiff with disapproval.

Proving to Ellie she was a better actress than she would have given herself credit for!

Not that that helped in the least now that she was left alone with her feelings. Part of her wanted to run after Patrick, to tell him that she had made a mistake, that it hadn't been an act on her part at all, that she wanted him with a desperation that made her shake with longing, in any sort of relationship he cared to choose.

But she did none of those things. Slowly she collected her coat from the closet, able to hear the murmur of voices upstairs—Tess's lightly teasing one, Patrick deep baritone—as she let herself out of the house.

It was beginning already, she realised as she drove numbly through the busy streets, totally immune to the Christmas gaiety in the shops around her. Toby was moving away to become a part of the McGrath family, to be enveloped in their warmth.

Something that, after today, Ellie knew she would never be...

CHAPTER ELEVEN

'IT's official, sis,' Toby announced happily as he came into the house Friday evening, throwing his outer coat over a chair as usual. 'Tess and I went out and bought the ring at lunchtime today,' he explained brightly as Ellie turned from cooking their evening meal to give him a questioning look.

She had been expecting it, had thought she had prepared herself for it, but as the sinking feeling increased in her stomach Ellie knew that she hadn't been ready for it at all.

It was all happening so quickly now that the decision had been made. Toby had dined with Thomas and Anne McGrath the previous evening, in order to ask Tess's father's permission for the two of them to marry. In view of Patrick's favourable opinion of Toby Ellie had known there would be no objection to the request, and there hadn't been. The McGraths were absolutely thrilled for their daughter, welcoming Toby into their family as if he were another son. Which, indeed, he would be.

Whereas Ellie still hadn't quite come to terms with the fact that she wasn't so much losing a brother as gaining the McGrath family. One member of the McGrath family in particular!

As she had expected, after their last conversation she had heard nothing from Patrick since they'd parted so abruptly on Wednesday morning. It had been a very long three days!

'The engagement party is going to be at the McGraths' on Christmas Eve,' Toby continued chattily, as he uncorked the bottle of champagne he had brought in with him and took three glasses out of the cupboard.

The engagement party…!

Ellie was filled with a mass of contradictions at the thought of seeing Patrick again. Happiness, because she ached to see him, and despair, because seeing him again would do nothing to alleviate that ache. Besides, he might actually be at the party with someone!

'That's wonderful, Toby.' She pushed aside her own feelings to give her brother a congratulatory hug. 'I'm really pleased for you both,' she added with total sincerity, taking the glass of pink champagne her brother handed her. 'To you and Tess,' she toasted warmly.

Toby took a sip of the champagne before lifting up his own glass. 'To the best Christmas ever,' he returned with feeling.

Ellie took another sip of her drink. Christmas. Despite knowing that it was quickly looming, she hadn't really given it much thought. But now that Toby was engaged to Tess it posed the problem of whether she and Toby would actually even celebrate Christmas together this year.

Christmas always tended to be rather a quiet affair for the two of them anyway, with them having no really close relatives. It promised to be even quieter than usual for Ellie this year!

'We're both invited to spend Christmas with the

McGraths too,' Toby informed her as he turned to pick up the bottle of champagne and replenish their glasses.

Ellie was relieved that her brother was actually turning away as he made this announcement, otherwise he wouldn't have failed to notice the look of complete dismay that she wasn't quick enough to hide.

Christmas with the McGraths. With Patrick.

Much as Ellie longed to see him, to be with him, she hated the thought of being invited to spend Christmas with his family as if she were some sort of charity case!

'It's very nice of them to ask me, Toby,' she said slowly, at the same time shaking her head. 'But I really don't think—'

'If you don't go, sis, then neither do I,' her brother told her with a frown.

Blackmail. Of the emotional kind. But not deviously so; Ellie knew it was only that Toby just wouldn't be happy leaving her here on her own over the Christmas period. Even if she would have preferred it!

She drew in a controlling breath. 'Perhaps for Christmas lunch,' she conceded reluctantly.

'I understand the invitation is for the whole of the Christmas period,' drawled an all too familiar voice from behind her.

Ellie turned sharply to look at Patrick as he stood in the doorway. She really would have to get a lock put on that door, one that came into effect automatically as it closed. In fact several of them, just to be sure!

'We were just drinking a toast to Tess and our engagement.' Toby felt none of the dismay at Patrick's presence that Ellie did, turning to pour some of the bubbly champagne into the third glass he had put out on the work surface.

Three glasses. Which meant Toby had already been aware that the other man was about to join them...

'Cheers.' Patrick toasted the younger man before sipping the champagne. But his gaze, enigmatic over the rim of his glass, remained firmly fixed on Ellie. Who just continued to stare back at him. Toby had obviously known the other man was coming here this evening, but for what reason?

Toby put his empty glass down on the worktop. 'I'm just going upstairs to change; I won't be long.'

'Not exactly subtle, is he?' Patrick drawled ruefully once Toby could be heard going up the stairs two at a time. Patrick was wearing a dark overcoat over the suit he had obviously worn to work, flecks of the gentle snow falling outside had settled on his shoulders and in the darkness of his hair.

Ellie had recovered from some of her shock at Patrick being here, although she was still slightly puzzled as to why he was there at all. 'Does he need to be?' she said guardedly, feeling decidedly casual in her worn denims and sloppy old blue jumper. Patrick gave a shrug. 'I thought I would come and add my—voice to my parents' invitation for you to spend Christmas with all of us.'

His voice? What did that mean, exactly?

He sighed, putting down his glass, the champagne only half drunk. 'Ellie, I realise that you probably don't want to spend Christmas with me, of all people, but if I try to keep my presence down to a minimum will you at least think about it?'

'There's really no need—' She swallowed hard, touched by his offer in spite of the fact that he had it all wrong—he was exactly the person she would love to spend Christmas with! Just not under these circumstances. 'It's very kind of your parents to make the offer,' she said non-committally.

His mouth twisted into a humourless smile. 'They really do want to meet you, Ellie,' he assured her dryly.

She shrugged. 'I'm sure there will be plenty of opportunity for that at the engagement party.'

'Hmm,' Patrick conceded slowly. 'Ellie, about the engagement party...'

She looked up at him sharply, tensing defensively as she guessed by his guarded expression that he was about to say something she wasn't going to like. 'Yes?' she prompted warily.

'Look, would you mind if I took my coat off? It's very warm in here,' he added, even as he shrugged out of the thick outer coat.

Ellie's wariness deepened. Obviously Patrick wasn't in any particular hurry to leave this evening, and dinner was quite obviously cooking away quite happily on top of the stove, a roast chicken was in the oven; the last thing she wanted was to feel compelled by good manners to ask him to join them for dinner. She would probably choke on the chicken!

'You were saying?' she prompted sharply.

Patrick picked up his champagne glass, emptying it in one swallow before looking across at her once more. 'It's going to be a big family party.' He grimaced. 'Brothers, sisters, aunts, uncles—and cousins,' he added pointedly.

Meaning Sarah and Gareth would undoubtedly be there…

'What I'm trying to say, Ellie,' Patrick continued impatiently, 'is do you think you could bury your hostility for one evening and come to the party as my partner?'

'Hostility…?' she echoed faintly, knowing exactly why he had made the invitation, but knowing a sense of inner excitement anyway. If he were inviting her to be his partner on Christmas Eve, then he obviously wasn't taking anyone else…

But did he really think she viewed him with hostility? When it was taking every ounce of will power she possessed not to throw herself into his arms and kiss him until they were both senseless? It was a weakness she had no intention of giving in to!

'I don't feel in the least hostile towards you, Patrick,' she told him crisply, at the same time giving a firm shake of her head. 'I have no idea why you should even think that I do.' Unless…? Tess wouldn't have told her brother of those remarks of Ellie's she had overheard, would she? She knew that the brother and sister were close, but it would be rather silly of her future sister-in-law if she had; it certainly wasn't guaranteed to further the smooth running of inter-family relations.

Patrick's mouth twisted into a self-derisive grimace. 'You were pretty—forceful in expressing your feelings towards me the other morning.'

But surely not to the point where he'd thought she felt hostility towards him?

She frowned. 'I believe I admitted to there being a certain—attraction between us—'

Patrick nodded. 'At the same time as you told me you still have feelings for Davies!' he bit out harshly.

Well…yes, she had hinted at something like that. But what else could she have done, in the circumstances? She still felt battered and bruised from Gareth's totally mercenary betrayal two months ago; wasn't she allowed a little self-pride now?

'Let's leave Gareth out of this,' she suggested abruptly.

'I would be pleased never even to hear the man's name again,' Patrick assured her harshly, his face set in grim lines. 'Unfortunately, that isn't yet possible. He and Sarah will be at the party on Christmas Eve; there's absolutely no doubt about that. In the circumstances, I think it would be—politically correct if you were there as my partner.' His eyes was narrowed on her compellingly.

Politically correct. How Ellie hated the phrase that seemed to have become so popular over the last few years. But in this case she could see how adequately it described the situation they found themselves in.

Her mouth twisted ruefully. 'Not the most gracious invitation I've ever received,' she mocked lightly. 'But if you think it will be of any help, of course I'll come as your partner.' It wasn't a completely unselfish decision; she hadn't particularly relished the idea of being at the party on her own anyway.

The tension seemed to ease out of Patrick's shoulders, his expression relaxing into a self-derisive smile. 'Not the most gracious acceptance of an invitation *I've* ever received either—but I suppose it will have to do,' he added dryly.

Ellie eyed him uncertainly, not quite knowing what to say next. Patrick seemed to be having the same problem, and the air of tension deepened between the two of them, with only the sound of the saucepans boiling on the stove to breach the silence.

Pointedly so, it seemed to Ellie, and if it were anyone else but Patrick she would already have invited them to stay to dinner…

Thankfully Toby chose that moment to come bouncing back into the kitchen, changed now into an Aran sweater and a pair of black denims. But he seemed to lose some of his bounce as he noticed the food cooking.

'Did I forget to mention that Tess and I are going out to dinner at a Chinese restaurant this evening?' He grimaced guiltily.

No, Ellie instantly realised with dismay, Toby hadn't forgotten to mention it at all—she was the one who was so muddle-headed at the moment that she had forgotten he had ever told her!

Going to work had become a nightmare, never knowing whether or not she might accidentally bump into Gareth and so be a victim of more of his veiled threats, and life at home didn't feel much better at the moment—she was either pining because she wasn't seeing Patrick, or a trembling mass of nerves when she did. Not a good inducement to remembering anything that was said to her.

Toby glanced at the bubbling saucepans. 'Perhaps Patrick—'

'Go, Toby,' his boss and future brother-in-law cut in decisively.

'But—'

'If your sister wants to invite me to share her evening meal, then I'm sure she will do so.' Patrick sharply interrupted Toby once again. 'Don't bully her into it, okay?' he added, more gently.

'Okay.' Toby shrugged, as if he couldn't quite see what the problem was but didn't have the time right now to try and find out. 'I'll see you later, then, sis.' He moved to kiss her lightly on the cheek. 'I really am sorry about the meal.' He grimaced again in apology, raising a hand in parting to Patrick before hurrying out of the house.

The silence after his departure was even more tense. Except for those bubbling saucepans, Ellie acknowledged impatiently.

'I had better—'

'Would you—?'

They both began talking at once, both breaking off at the same time too.

'After you,' Ellie invited with a rueful shrug.

'Ladies first,' Patrick insisted.

She didn't want to go first, positive that Patrick had been about to say he had better be leaving, whereas she—through sheer good manners—had been about to invite him to share her evening meal. Something she was sure Patrick was well aware of, which was why he was suggesting she go first! Although why on earth he should want to stay and have dinner with her Ellie had no idea...

She drew in a deep breath. 'I was about to suggest that you join me for dinner. It seems a pity to waste the roast chicken,' she added dismissively.

Patrick continued to look at her for several seconds.

Then his mouth began to twitch, and finally he burst out laughing. He finally sobered enough to speak, eyes sparkling with humour. 'You know, Ellie, you do absolutely nothing for my ego. ''It seems a pity to waste the roast chicken'',' he repeated incredulously, before he began to laugh again. Ellie looked at him frowningly for several seconds, before she also saw the funny side of it. She had sounded distinctly uninterested in his answer, to the point of rudeness. In fact, it was to Patrick's credit that he could laugh about it.

'I'll try again, shall I?' she decided self-derisively. 'Patrick, I would like it very much if you would join me for dinner,' she amended ruefully.

Patrick sobered, but his eyes still laughed as he looked across at her. 'Truthfully?' he prompted sceptically.

'Truthfully,' she echoed huskily.

It might be a mistake on her part, a self-indulgence that she would later regret, but at this moment, after several days of not seeing or hearing from him, she could think of nothing she wanted more than to spend the evening with Patrick. Anything to stop him leaving just yet.

'Then I accept.' He nodded teasingly. 'The roast chicken smells wonderful,' he added. 'Much better than the frozen lasagna I was going to put in the microwave when I got home!'

Ellie moved to take the vegetables off the cooker. 'Do you cater for yourself a lot?' she prompted interestedly, relieved to have an innocuous subject to talk about. Although, no matter how hard she tried, she couldn't quite see Patrick wandering round a supermarket buying his weekly groceries!

'Sometimes.' Patrick nodded. 'Is there anything I can do to help?' he offered as she began to serve the meal.

She opened her mouth to refuse, and then thought better of it; a busy Patrick wouldn't be able to sit and watch her as she carved the chicken and served the vegetables. 'There's knives and forks in the drawer under the table. Salt and pepper in the cupboard over there,' she accepted lightly.

It was strangely intimate, moving about the kitchen together, with Patrick pouring some more of the champagne to accompany their meal once he had set the kitchen table.

Something else Ellie was sure Patrick didn't normally do. No doubt he usually ate in the dining room in his own home. Well, they didn't have a dining room as such—the house wasn't big enough for such a luxury.

'This reminds me of when I was a child,' Patrick told her happily as they sat down to eat their meal. 'My nanny used to serve tea in the nursery when I was home from boarding school,' he explained at Ellie's questioning look. 'I was less than pleased when I reached the age of twelve and my parents decided I was grown up enough to eat in the formal dining room with them. No fun at all,' he added with a grimace.

Ellie eyed him interestedly. 'Did you enjoy going to boarding school?' Their lives, their upbringing, really had been so different.

'Not particularly,' he dismissed. 'It was just the done thing, I suppose.' He shrugged. 'My father and grandfather went there before me—that sort of thing.' He frowned. 'That particular tradition will end with my own children, I'm afraid; I have no intention of educating them away from home.'

His children. He spoke about having them so easily that he must have given the subject some thought.

Whereas Ellie found the thought of Patrick's children—children he would have with some as yet unnamed other woman—highly displeasing!

'Mmm, Ellie, this food is delicious!' Patrick broke enthusiastically into her disturbing thoughts, having just tasted the roast chicken. 'Where on earth did you learn to cook like this?' he complimented warmly.

Her cheeks became flushed with pleasure at the obvious sincerity of his compliments. 'My mother and my grandmother before me, I suppose,' she returned lightly.

'Thank you, Mother and Grandmother!' He raised his glass in a toast. 'When Toby moves out, can I move in?' he added hopefully.

He was only joking, Ellie knew he was, and yet just the thought of it deepened the blush in her cheeks. What would it be like, living with Patrick all the time? Talking with him, laughing with him, making love with him? Heaven, she decided wistfully.

And just as quickly pushed the thought very firmly from her mind!

'Wouldn't it be easier to just hire yourself a cook?' she suggested derisively.

'It might,' he conceded slowly. 'But, again, not as much fun,' he added with a smile.

Ellie eyed him interestedly. 'You seem to put great store on having fun…?'

Patrick shrugged. 'If you aren't enjoying what you're doing, or who you're with, there doesn't seem to be much point in pursuing it. Does there?' he reasoned huskily.

Did that mean he enjoyed being with her? That he wouldn't be here at all, wouldn't have accepted her invitation, if that weren't the case?

That did seem to be what he was saying. But Ellie knew she must try to keep remembering that Patrick's only interest in her lay in ensuring the happiness of his much younger sister...

Besides, he could just be warning her of how stupid she was to continue to have feelings for Gareth!

How she wished she had never made that claim! It had seemed the only thing to do at the time, had been done completely out of self-defence. But a part of her still wished Patrick hadn't believed the outright lie...

'Not everyone has the luxury of such choices,' she told him hardly.

Patrick gave her a considering look. 'Is working at Delacorte, Delacorte and Delacorte still proving difficult?'

Impossible would probably better describe this last week. In fact, she was seriously thinking of changing her job. Maybe it was time she moved on anyway; she had worked for the same company for almost ten years now. Her home life would be changing radically when Toby and Tess were married and her brother moved away from home, so maybe it was time for her to move on too?

She turned away from Patrick's probing eyes. 'I'm sure you can have no real interest in hearing about my problems,' she dismissed lightly. 'Your food is getting cold,' she reminded him as he would have spoken.

Patrick continued to look at her wordlessly for several long seconds before giving an abrupt inclination of his head. 'So it is.'

The silence that followed as they began to eat— Patrick with obvious enjoyment, Ellie less than enthusiastically—was no more reassuring than his probing questions had been.

She could sense there was still so much Patrick would have liked to say to her, but didn't. And it was the content of what he had left unsaid that troubled her now.

'That was excellent, Ellie,' Patrick told her warmly as he finished his meal.

She stood up to clear the plates; Patrick's was completely empty, her own food was only half eaten. 'I'm afraid we don't usually bother with dessert,' she explained with a grimace.

'I don't eat them, anyway.' He sat back in his chair to look across at her. 'Ellie, do you think—?' He broke off as a knock sounded on the back door, his body tensing, his eyes narrowing coldly as Gareth opened the door and entered the kitchen.

Ellie stared at the other man in total disbelief.

What on earth was Gareth doing here?

CHAPTER TWELVE

GARETH didn't look surprised to see the other man sitting in the kitchen with Ellie, and she quickly realised that was because he must have seen the Mercedes parked outside in the driveway and drawn his own conclusions as to its owner being Patrick.

Which posed the question: why had Gareth come here, knowing that Patrick was already there?

In fact, why had Gareth come here at all?

Not that the why really mattered; one look at the suspicion that now narrowed Patrick's eyes, the disgusted twist on his lips as he slowly stood up, was enough to tell Ellie that he had drawn his own conclusions as to the reason Gareth was here.

Ellie felt her heart plummet at the realisation. It was one thing for her to actually claim—falsely!—to have residual feelings towards Gareth, something else entirely for Gareth to come here and so give Patrick the impression that there might be more to it than that.

Gareth gave a confident smile. 'Patrick,' he greeted him lightly. 'Ellie,' he added warmly.

With Patrick's broodingly disapproving attention all focused on the other man, Ellie felt free to glare her resentment across the kitchen at Gareth. He looked so completely unconcerned at her obvious lack of welcome, so sure of himself, that a part of her just wanted to wipe that slightly mocking smile off his too-handsome face!

He raised mocking brows at her obviously glowering expression. 'I didn't have a chance to see you before you left the office earlier, so I just popped in to wish you a merry Christmas,' he told her with a challenging smile.

A merry—! What on earth was Gareth up to? With Christmas just under a week away, Delacorte, Delacorte and Delacorte had finished for a two-week Christmas holiday at five o'clock this evening. Ellie had decided to give the usual impromptu office party a miss this year, mainly in an effort to avoid seeing Gareth and so completely ruining her day. With his arrival here instead, she realised she might as well have saved herself the bother!

'You could have done that on Christmas Eve.' Patrick was the one to answer the other man harshly. 'My parents are having a party that evening to celebrate my sister Teresa's engagement to Ellie's brother Toby; you and Sarah are obviously invited,' he explained scathingly.

Uncertainty flickered briefly in Gareth's eyes at what was obviously news to him, to be quickly masked as he once again smiled confidently. 'Of course,' he said smoothly. 'But parties can be so impersonal, can't they? And Ellie and I used to be such close friends,' he added pointedly.

Not *that* sort of 'close friends'! Thank goodness. This situation would be even more humiliating if she and Gareth *had* ever been lovers!

'Champagne?' Gareth's gaze narrowed as he noticed

the empty bottle standing on one of the worktops. 'The two of *you* wouldn't have something to celebrate too, would you?' he added, with a conspiratorially knowing look in Ellie's direction.

He really believed that she and Toby were no better than he was, she realised angrily. 'Only Toby and Teresa's engagement,' she snapped coldly.

'Of course,' Gareth acknowledged smoothly.

Too smoothly for Ellie's liking. Why didn't he just go? He had obviously succeeded in what he'd come here to do, namely create a difficult situation for Ellie where Patrick was concerned, so why didn't he just leave? Surely there wasn't more to come…?

'Looks like we're all going to be one big happy family, doesn't it,' Gareth continued pleasantly.

'Two out of the three, perhaps,' Patrick rasped icily. 'And in your case I wouldn't be too sure about the third one either!' He gave the young man a scathing glance.

Gareth looked at Patrick consideringly. 'I get the distinct feeling that you don't particularly like me…' he murmured slowly, at the same time somehow managing to sound like a hurt little boy.

Not that Patrick looked particularly impressed by the latter, Ellie noted ruefully.

What she really wanted now was for both men to just leave. Her nerves were stretched to breaking point after the last hour or so, and Gareth's arrival a few minutes ago was doing nothing to help that situation. In fact, she was starting to feel decidedly ill, not knowing from one moment to the next what Gareth was going to say. Patrick either, for that matter. The two men looked like a pair of gladiators, facing each other across the arena!

'I've never liked men who feel the need to beat up women,' said Patrick disgustedly, hands clenched into fists at his sides as he glared at the other man.

'Beat—? Ellie?' Gareth scowled as he turned to look at her. 'What on earth have you been telling Patrick about me?' He looked slightly less confident now.

'She didn't need to tell me anything,' Patrick assured him coldly. 'I've seen the bruises you inflicted on her the night of the company dinner, and at my aunt and uncle's house the following evening! Next time you feel like threatening someone, come and see me, hmm?' He looked challengingly at the younger man.

As far as Ellie was concerned, this situation was rapidly spiralling out of control; if she didn't put a stop to it right now she had a feeling the two of them might actually start fighting in the middle of her kitchen!

She stepped forward, effectively standing between the two men. 'You've said what you came here to say, Gareth,' she rasped—done what he wanted to do! 'Now I suggest you leave.'

He continued to hold Patrick's gaze for several more long seconds, before giving a slight inclination of his head. 'I'll look forward to seeing you both on Christmas Eve, then.' he shrugged dismissively.

'Don't hold your breath on that one either,' Patrick bit out harshly as the other man left.

Gareth paused to turn in the doorway and look back at them. 'Sarah and I have set our wedding date for Easter weekend,' he drawled mockingly.

'A lot can happen in three and a half months,' Patrick replied calmly.

Gareth gave a derisive grin. 'Who knows? Maybe

you and Ellie will decide to make it a double wedding!' he taunted, his smile one of satisfaction as he saw Ellie's embarrassed dismay at the outrageous suggestion. 'See you,' he added lightly, before letting himself out.

If she had thought the situation tense before Gareth's arrival, Ellie now felt as if she could cut the atmosphere with a knife. Gareth was nothing but an arrogant, troublemaking—

Patrick spoke forcefully into that tense silence. 'I will never—never, *ever*,' he continued with feeling, 'understand what either Sarah or you see in that man!' His mouth twisted with distaste, his eyes still cold with the dislike he didn't even attempt to hide.

As far as Ellie was concerned, she saw Gareth exactly as Patrick did. But she knew she would just be wasting her time to try and tell him that now—could see by the scorn on his face that he wouldn't believe her.

Patrick gave an impatient shake of his head. 'I think I should leave now,' he rasped, taking his overcoat from the back of the chair. 'Do you want me to collect you on Christmas Eve, or will you drive over with Toby?' he added uninterestedly.

What Ellie most wanted to do right now was sit down and have a good cry. And once Patrick had gone that was exactly what she was going to do. In fact, if he didn't soon leave she might just break down and cry in front of him!

'I'll come over with Toby,' she answered quietly, looking down at the tiled floor in preference to Patrick's scornful expression.

'Fine,' he snapped harshly. 'I— Thanks for dinner,' he added, with a slight softening of his tone.

That slight relenting on Patrick's part was her undoing. The tears started to fall hotly down her cheeks, a sob catching in the back of her throat as those tears threatened to choke her.

'Hey,' Patrick murmured gently as he saw those tears, throwing his overcoat back down on the chair to come over stand in front of Ellie. 'He isn't worth it, you know,' he added dismissively, his hand moving to lift her chin and raise her face so that he could look at her.

The tears fell more rapidly because she knew he had misunderstood the reason for them, but also knew she couldn't correct him without losing all the ground she had gained in the last few days; it would be just too humiliating if Patrick were to realise her tears were because she was in love with him, and not Gareth, as he supposed!

'Why is it that nice women seem to fall in love with bastards?' Patrick rasped, with a disgusted shake of his head.

She shrugged. 'Sarah is still very young—'

'I was referring to you!' Patrick cut in harshly, grey eyes glittering coldly.

Ellie blinked, looking up at him uncertainly. 'Am I a nice woman…?'

'Of course you are,' he confirmed impatiently. 'One of the nicest I've ever met,' he assured her hardly. 'In fact, the only thing that's wrong with you is this tendency you have to be in love with the wrong man!'

She gave a choked laugh. 'The only thing…?'

Patrick gave an impatient snort. 'Ridiculous, isn't it?' he dismissed disgustedly. 'But I'll tell you one thing, Ellie,' he snapped decisively. 'After speaking to the man this evening, I'm even more convinced that Gareth Davies marries Sarah over my dead body!'

Ellie looked up at him searchingly. What about her? How would he feel about *her* marrying Gareth? Not that it was even a possibility, but she couldn't help noticing Patrick's omission where she was concerned…

Patrick returned her gaze for several long minutes, finally releasing her chin to take a step away from her. 'Once I've sorted that particular situation out,' he said grimly, pulling on his overcoat, 'I'm going to do everything in my power to ensure *you* don't marry him either!'

She swallowed hard. 'You are?'

'Most definitely,' he assured her determinedly. 'There is absolutely no way that man is going to become part of my family—even by marriage!'

Oh. Patrick's vehemence had nothing to do with her personally. He just wanted to ensure Gareth had nothing to do with the McGrath family.

She grimaced. 'You'll have more trouble convincing Sarah of that than me!'

'We'll see,' he came back enigmatically. 'You're sure you don't want me to pick you up on Christmas Eve?'

'Positive,' she assured him with feeling.

He nodded impatiently. 'I'll see you in a few days, then?'

'Yes,' she confirmed.

Why didn't he just go now? He had made it more

than plain exactly what his interest was in her and her supposed feelings for Gareth, so why didn't he just leave?

Before she started to cry again!

Patrick shook his head frustratedly as he continued looked down at her tear-stained face. 'I could kiss you until you're senseless!' he muttered harshly.

Ellie's eyes widened. 'What would that achieve?' she finally murmured huskily.

'Absolutely nothing,' he accepted impatiently. 'But it would make me feel a whole lot better!'

And it would reduce her to a complete emotional puddle!

She straightened defensively. 'I don't think so, thank you, Patrick,' she told him evenly.

His mouth twisted humourlessly. 'No, neither do I.' He sighed, turning without another word and letting himself out of the house, closing the door gently behind him as he left.

Ellie's shoulders slumped once she was alone.

How much more of this would she have to take? How much more of this could she be expected to take?

CHAPTER THIRTEEN

'TOBY, could you zip me up—?' Ellie's words came to an abrupt halt as she entered the sitting room and found not Toby sitting there, as she had expected, but Patrick. She quickly turned fully to face him, clutching the front of her black dress to her chest. 'I thought Toby was in here...' she murmured self-consciously.

When had Patrick arrived? She hadn't heard the doorbell ring. Although, come to think of it, he hadn't rung the doorbell the last few times he'd arrived here unexpectedly either!

'He was, but he had to leave early so that he can be at the house with Teresa when the first guests arrive.' Patrick put down the magazine he had been idly flicking through when Ellie entered the room and stood up. 'You mentioned you have a zip that needs fastening...?' he prompted expectantly, once again suave and sophisticated himself, in a black dinner suit and snowy white shirt.

That had been before she'd realised it was Patrick in the room and not Toby!

'I'll manage,' she frowned. 'Okay, I understand about Toby, but what exactly are you doing here?' If Toby had told her he had to be at the McGraths earlier than arranged then she could quite easily have been ready in time to go with him. She was also quite capable of calling herself a taxi.

Patrick shrugged dismissively. 'I told you. It was decided that Toby should be with Teresa when the first guests arrive—'

'I understood that bit,' Ellie dismissed impatiently. 'I'm just not sure who decided you should be here.' She frowned.

'Does it matter?' Patrick dismissed uninterestedly.

Ellie gave a puzzled shake of her head; this present arrangement really didn't make much sense.

'Turn around and let me do up your zip,' Patrick instructed dryly.

Her hand tightened on the material she held up in front of her. It was yet another new dress, a figure-hugging black tube that seemed to cling to her body magnetically, having neither shoulder straps nor sleeves to keep it in place, leaving her legs long and shapely beneath its knee length.

'I said turn around, Ellie,' he repeated encouragingly.

She wore neither bra nor slip beneath the dress, just a pair of black lace panties, the top of which would be clearly visible if she turned around, as the zip unfastened down the whole length of her spine.

But she could see by Patrick's face that he wasn't about to be fobbed off with an excuse, and sighed heavily as she slowly turned her back towards him.

Nothing happened for several long seconds. Ellie finally looked back over her shoulder to see what the problem was.

Patrick was looking across at her with dark eyes, his expression remotely unreadable, but a nerve pulsing erratically in his tightly clenched jaw.

Ellie turned quickly away again. 'We're going to be

late ourselves if we don't leave soon,' she encouraged huskily, finding she was trembling slightly now, unsure what to make of that look on Patrick's face. In any other man she would have said it was—But Patrick was like no other man she had ever met!

She gave a sensitive start as she felt the light touch of his fingers on the base of her spine, her back stiffening defensively at her unbidden response.

His fingertips slowly travelled the length of her spine, Ellie's skin seeming to burn where he touched, stopping as they reached the sensitised arch between her shoulderblades.

What was he doing? Ellie wondered with a mixture of pleasure and dismay. Pleasure because she liked his touch upon her naked flesh, dismay because the involuntary arching of her body must have told him how much she liked it!

His hands lightly gripped the tops of her shoulders, his thumbtips now moving in a slow caress against her spine and up the silky length of her neck.

Ellie swallowed hard, not sure how much more of this she could stand without turning in his arms and kissing him. Which would nullify everything she had done this last week to put a certain amount of distance between them.

'The zip, Patrick,' she reminded him determinedly, her jaw clenched in tight control now.

'Your skin feels so wonderful to the touch,' he murmured admiringly, seeming not to have heard her. Or, if he had, choosing to ignore her! 'But then I always knew that it would,' he continued gruffly. 'When I saw you in the garden, that day in the summer—'

'Never mind. I'll do the zip up myself!' Ellie said sharply, and she moved abruptly away to turn and glare at him. 'I think it's decidedly ungentlemanly of you to even mention seeing me that day in the garden!' she told him indignantly, eyes glowing deeply blue, her cheeks fiery-red with embarrassment.

Why, oh, why, couldn't Patrick just pretend not to remember seeing her sunbathing topless? It certainly wasn't the first time he had mentioned it!

She gave a low groan in her throat. 'I'll be back down in a few minutes!' She turned and fled the room before Patrick could even think of preventing her.

This was awful. Just awful. And it was only the beginning of the Christmas holiday—a holiday she had finally allowed Toby to persuade her into spending with the McGrath family. What choice did she have when Toby had refused to go if she didn't?

But it was going to be three days of hell if Patrick didn't hold to his promise to keep his distance!

'Ready?' he prompted lightly when she rejoined him downstairs a few minutes later.

Ellie eyed him warily, the black pashmina he had bought for her now brought back out of its box at the back of her wardrobe, draped about the nakedness of her shoulders. 'There's just my case and that bag to take with us,' she answered slowly, nodding in the direction of the two pieces of luggage she had brought down with her and left in the hallway.

Patrick bent down and picked up Ellie's case and the bag containing the impersonal Christmas presents she had bought for the McGrath family, straightening to grin at her. 'This feels almost indiscreet, don't you think?' He quirked dark brows. 'Almost as if the two of us are sneaking off somewhere together for the weekend,' he explained teasingly at her frowning look.

The warmth in her cheeks seemed to be becoming a permanent fixture! 'I really wouldn't know anything about that,' Ellie told him sharply; he probably had more experience with clandestine weekends away than she did. How could he not? Her own experience in that direction was precisely nil! 'I just need to check round the house once more before I leave to make sure I've switched everything off.' It really wouldn't do for the house to burn down in her three-day absence!

Patrick nodded. 'I'll put your things in the car while you do that.'

Ellie breathed more easily once he had left the room, moving slowly to double-check that she had switched off all the Christmas lights. As usual the tree looked starkly gaudy without its glittering lights. Ellie gazed up at it sadly as she accepted that by the time she returned to the house in three days' time Christmas would effectively be over.

It was strange to think—

What on earth was that?

She could hear raised voices outside, and they certainly didn't sound like the happy revellers she had been hearing the last few evenings; these voices sounded distinctly angry.

They also, she realised incredulously, sounded like Patrick and Gareth!

Ellie hurried from the sitting room, through the kitchen and out onto the driveway—arriving just in time to see Patrick punch Gareth on the chin!

She came to an abrupt halt, staring in horrified fascination as Gareth reeled from the blow but remained standing on his feet, only to swing his own fist up and land a punch in Patrick's right eye.

What on earth—?

Patrick also remained standing on his feet, his expression cold with fury as his arm swung once again.

'Patrick!' Ellie cried out in alarm. The sound of her voice caught both men off-guard and they turned to look at her.

But not quickly enough to stop Patrick's fist once again making contact with Gareth's chin. And this time he went down, falling heavily onto the concreted driveway, despite the thin layer of snow that still partially covered it.

'What do you think you're doing?' She hurried over to both men. The air seemed to pulse with their fury as she looked from one to the other of them.

Gareth still sat on the driveway, his hand raised to his bruised chin as he glared up balefully at the other man. Patrick was standing over him, his hands clenched into fists at his sides.

Ellie drew in a ragged breath, still not quite able to believe this was happening. 'I said—'

'Don't try and pretend you aren't as much a part of this as your boyfriend!' Gareth scorned, getting slowly to his feet now, dusting the snow from his denims as he did so.

'Leave Ellie out of it,' Patrick rasped harshly. 'In fact, why don't you just leave?' he added scathingly.

Gareth shook his head, his eyes narrowed with dislike as he looked at the older man. 'I'm not going anywhere,' he said slowly.

'No, you're not, are you?' Patrick acknowledged with satisfaction.

Ellie looked at both men as she felt the tension rising between them once more; any minute now they were going to start hitting each other again! 'Would someone please tell me exactly what is going on?' she demanded determinedly.

Gareth's mouth twisted derisively. 'Did the two of you think I would just take this lying down? Because, if you did, I can assure you—'

'You seemed to be doing a fair imitation of doing exactly that a few seconds ago!'

Patrick was antagonizing him. Almost as if, Ellie realised dazedly, he *wanted* the other man to take another swing at him—just so that he had a good excuse to hit Gareth again!

An angry red tide of colour moved into Gareth's cheeks. 'You—'

'Will you both stop this?' Ellie ordered impatiently. 'This happens to be my home. And, if nothing else, you're giving my neighbours something to gossip about all over Christmas!'

She had already seen the curtains twitching in the house opposite, the couple that lived there no doubt alerted to the fight outside by the sound of raised voices. As she had been...

'If you really must continue this—argument,' she bit out caustically, 'then at least come inside and do it. But don't even think about hitting each other again once we're in the house,' she warned as she turned to go inside. 'I don't want anything of mine broken!'

Anything *else* of hers broken; her heart was already in pieces!

She still had no idea what had caused this flare-up in the ongoing dislike the two men had of each other, but she certainly intended getting an explanation—from one of them!—before the evening was over.

Thankfully the two men followed her into the house, and Ellie looked at them frowningly once they all stood in the sitting room. Gareth's expression was belligerent as he glared at the other man; Patrick's was one of quiet satisfaction. It was that latter expression that roused Ellie's curiosity the most... But it was to Gareth she expressed her next remark.

'What are you doing here?'

Even if she and Patrick left for the party right now they were going to arrive well past the given time of eight o'clock; Gareth, wearing denims and a thick Aran jumper, wasn't even dressed to go out for the evening yet.

'Letting your boyfriend know that as far as I'm concerned this is far from over,' Gareth answered, his jaw clenched.

Ellie really wished he would stop referring to Patrick as her boyfriend...!

Patrick eyed the younger man derisively. 'In what way is it not over, Davies?' he prompted challengingly. 'Unless I'm mistaken, George has given you three months' notice at Delacorte, Delacorte and Delacorte. Notice he has waived in lieu of never having to set eyes on you again! I believe your engagement to Sarah is likewise terminated. Permanently!'

His satisfaction was no longer quiet!

Ellie's eyes widened. When on earth had all this happened? Four days ago Gareth had definitely still been a junior partner with Delacorte, Delacorte and Delacorte, and his engagement to Sarah had seemed unshakeable too...

But there was no mistaking the fact that Gareth certainly wasn't wearing the right sort of clothes to attend Toby and Teresa's engagement party this evening...

Gareth's mouth twisted contemptuously. 'You both think you've been so clever, don't you? Did you really think I would just go quietly?' he scorned, shaking his head. 'For one thing, George has no reason to dismiss me other than a personal one, which in a court of law—'

'He doesn't need one,' Patrick cut in confidently. 'I'm surprised at you, Davies; you really should have read the small print on your contract of employment,' he taunted. 'It clearly states that three months' notice can be given, on either side, without prejudice, during your first year of employment. You've been with Delacorte, Delacorte and Delacorte how long now...?' he prompted pointedly.

Ellie could see by Gareth's stunned expression that he really *hadn't* been aware of that particular clause in his contract of employment.

'As for your engagement to Sarah,' Patrick continued derisively, 'I believe it's a woman's prerogative to change her mind?'

Gareth's expression was ugly now. 'With a lot of help from her interfering family!' he rasped.

'Maybe.' Patrick shrugged unconcernedly. 'It doesn't change the fact that Sarah *has* changed her mind.'

The relief Ellie felt on hearing this completely dispelled any doubts she might have had about having the two men fighting in her driveway in full view of her neighbours. She didn't care how Patrick had achieved it. All that mattered was that Sarah had escaped Gareth's mercenary clutches!

But Gareth's feelings about the broken engagement were obviously different, and as he turned on the other man. 'You self-satisfied—'

'I said there would be no fighting in here, Gareth!' Ellie told him firmly as he took a threatening step towards Patrick.

Gareth turned a furious blue gaze on her. 'As for you—'

'I believe I told you to leave Ellie out of this,' Patrick reminded him in a dangerously soft voice.

The younger man's hands were clenched into fists at his sides. 'From what I can tell she's already in this up to her pretty neck!' Gareth rasped, his gaze raking over her scathingly. 'I hope you realise he'll never marry you, Ellie,' he taunted with hard derision. 'The McGraths and the Delacortes believe themselves far too good for the likes of you and me!' he added bitterly.

Ellie swallowed hard as she felt the colour drain from her cheeks, at the same time desperately hoping that neither of these men had seen just how much Gareth's last remark had hurt her. Of course Patrick would never consider marrying her; it wasn't even a possibility. But

she could well have done without having that fact
thrown in her face. Especially by a man she so utterly
despised.

'How do you work that one out, Davies?' Patrick was
the one to answer the other man scornfully. 'Tonight
we're celebrating the engagement of Ellie's brother and
my sister!'

'An engagement isn't a marriage,' the other man
came back derisively, before turning to look pityingly
at Ellie once again. 'An affair even less so,' he warned
her mockingly.

'Get out,' she told Gareth shakily.

'Oh, I'm going,' he assured her, raising a hand to his
bruised jaw. 'But I'll be back,' he added softly.

'In that case, make sure it's me you come back at;
come near Ellie again and you'll find out how it feels
to be on the wrong side in a court of law,' Patrick
warned him coldly. 'Which I don't think would do a
great deal for the furtherance of your legal career,' he
added challengingly.

Gareth's cheeks flushed angrily. 'Don't threaten me,
McGrath,' he rasped.

But his tone held little conviction, Ellie noted; the
possibility of ending up as the defendant in a court of
law rather than the prosecuting lawyer—for what
charge was anybody's guess!—obviously didn't appeal
to Gareth one little bit, if the suddenly wary expression
on his face was anything to go by.

A fact which, by his next comment, Patrick had obviously noticed too. 'Davies, I think the best thing for
everyone is for you to just disappear back down whatever sewer you came out of,' he advised dismissively.

The ugly flush deepened in Gareth's cheeks as he turned to direct his next insult at Ellie. 'Give me a call when he's finished with you—you never know; I just might be interested in continuing where we left off!' With one last contemptuous glare in Patrick's direction he exited the room, the back door slamming noisily behind him seconds later as he left the house.

The awkward silence that followed his abrupt exit made Ellie squirm...!

What must Patrick think of her now?

CHAPTER FOURTEEN

'Is it my imagination, or does Patrick have what looks to be the beginnings of a very black eye?'

Ellie turned sharply at the sound of Sarah's voice. She had been looking at Patrick herself until that moment, as he stood across the room talking with one of his numerous aunts; Ellie had quickly learnt, on their arrival at the party an hour ago, that the McGrath family was a large one, and Patrick a particular favourite with all of them.

She looked up warily at Sarah now. 'Sorry?' she prompted guardedly.

Sarah's smile was a little strained, but other than that she looked as beautiful as ever in a short, figure-hugging red dress. 'Don't look so apprehensive about seeing me, please, Ellie.' She reached out and gave Ellie's arm a reassuring squeeze. 'After all, I believe we've both recently made a very lucky escape?' She quirked self-derisive brows.

Ellie grimaced. The problem was, she still didn't really have any idea what had happened to end Sarah's engagement to Gareth. It had been well after eight o'clock by the time Gareth made his furious exit from her house, and, other than pausing briefly to collect an ice-pack to place on Patrick's rapidly bruising eye, the two of them had come straight to the engagement party. Although, as Sarah had so astutely noticed, the ice pack didn't seem to have worked too well; Patrick definitely had the start of bruising that would be a very black eye!

'Yes,' she confirmed huskily. 'And, yes, Patrick does have a black eye.' She grimaced. In fact, by tomorrow, it would probably rival the bruises on her arm for all the colours of the rainbow! Gareth, when thwarted, really was a very violent man.

Sarah frowned across at her cousin. 'I suppose it's too much to hope that Gareth had nothing to do with it?'

Ellie sighed. 'I'm afraid it is.' She nodded.

Sarah shook her head, her gaze troubled as she looked at Ellie. 'How could two such accomplished women as us ever have been so stupid where Gareth was concerned?' she muttered disgustedly.

Ellie couldn't help it; she laughed. And, after several stunned seconds, so did Sarah, the two women falling weakly into each others arms as they laughed together.

'"Two such accomplished women as us"?' Ellie repeated as she finally straightened, aware that their laughter had a slightly hysterical edge to it. Also aware that they were attracting a certain amount of attention.

Sarah took two glasses of champagne from a passing waiter, handing one to Ellie. 'To liberation,' she toasted determinedly.

Whatever had happened to cause Sarah to break her engagement, Ellie was pleased to see that on the surface at least Sarah seemed to be recovering rapidly from the disappointment.

She couldn't help admiring the younger woman; it couldn't have been easy for Sarah to come here this evening. The announcement of her own engagement had only been made days ago—an engagement that had now been abruptly terminated.

'Liberation,' Ellie echoed just as firmly, before taking a sip of the bubbly wine. 'Sarah—'

'It really is all right, Ellie,' Sarah assured her with a smile that didn't quite light up her eyes. 'I'm still a little shell-shocked, obviously, but I'll get over it. How about you?'

Ellie shuddered. 'I got over Gareth months ago!' Only to fall irrevocably in love with Patrick!

'Hmm,' Sarah nodded ruefully. 'I believe I was mostly to blame for what happened to you—for—for—'

'Gareth dumping me?' Ellie finished dismissively. 'Yes, you were—thank goodness.' She gave a shake of her head. 'Gareth didn't—he didn't hurt you in any way, did he?' She frowned her concern.

The younger woman gave a humourless laugh. 'My pride,' she grimaced. 'I can't believe now that I ever thought he was so wonderful! Boy, did his true colours come out when I told him about the designs I had sent Jacques, and that I would like to delay the wedding for a while so that I could return to Paris for six months.' She gave a disgusted shake of her head. 'He seemed to think that you and Patrick had had a hand in it somewhere, which I found extremely puzzling to start with. But he kept going on about ''a woman scorned''—that you would say and do anything to try and break the two of us up. The penny finally dropped, and I realised that you and he must have been dating until I came back to England a couple of months ago. Why didn't you tell me, Ellie?' she chided gently. 'In your shoes,

I would have wanted to scratch the other woman's eyes out!'

Ellie gave a shake of her head. 'I knew what Gareth was really like by then, and if anything I wanted to try and warn you off him.'

Sarah took a sip of her champagne. 'So why didn't you?' she prompted curiously.

She glanced across to where Patrick was now in conversation with his parents. 'Patrick convinced me that you probably wouldn't believe me.' She grimaced.

'He did?' Sarah looked across at her cousin, blonde brows raised speculatively.

'Mmm,' Ellie nodded. 'So what did happen to—to change your mind about Gareth?'

Sarah gave another grimace. 'Well, I wasn't too happy with the things he said about you and Patrick. As you've probably realized, Patrick is a particular favourite with me, and, although we haven't seen a lot of each other this last year, you and I have been friends for a long time too,' she said. 'The things he said about the two of you were bad enough, but it was when he started insulting my father that I took exception!'

Ellie looked up at her disbelievingly. 'Your father?' Was Gareth completely stupid? Or, more to the point, so arrogant he didn't realise when he was stepping on dangerous ground?

Sarah gave a rueful smile. 'Never, ever insult the girl's father ought to be the first rule any man should learn about courtship!' She gave a self-conscious shake of her head. 'Ellie, I adore my father—'

'It's reciprocated,' she confirmed affectionately.

Sarah nodded. 'Gareth was obviously too stupid to

realise that,' she dismissed hardly. 'And all because he couldn't have his own way about the wedding!'

'You do realize why now, though?' Ellie prompted cautiously.

'Oh, yes,' Sarah acknowledged self-disgustedly. 'Don't worry, Ellie, my eyes are wide open now where Gareth Davies is concerned!'

'I'm very glad to hear it!' Patrick announced with satisfaction as he joined the two of them.

Ellie gave a nervous start, having been completely unaware of his approach. She looked up at him as he came to stand beside her. Yes, his eye was now turning a rather nice shade of purple.

He returned her gaze unblinkingly. 'How about you, Ellie, are your eyes wide open now too?'

About Gareth? Or did he mean something else...?

'I think we should put some raw steak on that eye,' she answered instead.

Sarah winced as she looked at him. 'Does it hurt?'

Patrick shrugged. 'Not as much as Davies's jaw, I expect,' he said with satisfaction.

His young cousin laughed. 'I hope you gave him a punch from me!'

Patrick grimaced. 'I think he may have a little trouble eating for a few days.'

'Good,' Sarah bit out firmly, before turning to Ellie and lightly squeezing her arm. 'I'm really glad the two of us have had this little chat together. But now, if the two of you will excuse me, I think I'll go over and tell my father how wonderful he is!' She gave a glowing smile.

'I'm sure Uncle George will be pleased about that,' Patrick encouraged huskily.

'I hope so.' Sarah laughed softly. 'I'll see you both later.'

There was a silence after Sarah had left to weave her way through the crowd to where her father stood talking to Patrick's parents. Although it wasn't a particularly awkward silence. More, Ellie decided, an expectant one...

'I'm sure there will be something in the fridge in the kitchen that I can put on this eye.' Patrick finally spoke huskily at Ellie's side. 'Care to come with me?'

Why not? The engagement had already been announced, and Toby and Teresa were the centre of attention as everyone stood around laughing and talking. The buffet supper was to be served in an hour's time.

'If you think I can be of help,' Ellie agreed.

Patrick gave her a considering look. 'I'm not really sure you're ready to hear what I'm thinking right now, Ellie.'

She looked up at him searchingly. Could she be mistaken, or had there been a wistful note in his voice just now?

She drew in a deep breath, swallowing hard before speaking. 'Patrick, exactly why did you come to my house this evening?'

He shrugged. 'Because I knew, once I was made aware that Sarah had finished things with Davies, that his next move would be to pay you a call.'

She had already worked that part out for herself! 'And?' she prompted huskily.

'Ellie, do you think we could get out of this crush of

people before I answer that?' he asked impatiently, not waiting for her answer but taking a firm hold of her arm to guide her out of the sitting room, through the hallway—beautifully decorated with boughs of holly and red ribbons—into the kitchen at the back of the house.

As Ellie had expected, the McGrath house was equally as grand as the Delacortes'. The huge kitchen was of mellow oak, with a dozen or more copper saucepans hanging from the rack over the work table in the centre of the room, and a green Aga giving the room its warmth.

Patrick grimaced as he saw there were several members of the household staff bustling around the room, preparing the last of the buffet supper. 'Is there nowhere in this house that we can be alone?'

He scowled his displeasure, whereas Ellie felt heartened by the fact that he wanted to talk to her alone!

'They've almost finished, Patrick,' she soothed lightly, giving one of the maids a sympathetic look as she glanced at them curiously. 'Why don't you see if there's any red meat in the fridge we can put on your eye?'

'Damn my eye!' he dismissed impatiently, grasping hold of her hand to pull her out of the room, back down the corridor and into another room off the hallway. 'Ah,' he said with satisfaction as he saw this room— probably his father's study, judging by the desk and book-lined walls—was empty. He closed the door behind them decisively, and the two of them were instantly surrounded by blessed silence.

Ellie eyed Patrick quizzically for several seconds. 'And?' she finally reminded him huskily.

He grimaced. 'I came over to your house this evening because—because—'

'Yes?' Ellie prompted breathlessly, a cautious excitement starting to build up inside her.

Patrick drew in a harsh breath. 'Because if Davies had come over to see you with the intention of hurting you in any way I intended stopping him,' he bit out determinedly, grimacing as Ellie continued to look at him wordlessly. 'Because if he'd come to see you with any intention of persuading you into taking him back into your life I intended stopping him from doing that too! As I told you I would,' he concluded impatiently, grey gaze challenging.

It was a challenge Ellie had no intention of answering. A hope was welling up inside her now, so intense that she could barely breathe, let alone speak.

'Ellie, don't you want to know the reason why?' Patrick finally asked harshly.

She thought—hoped!—she knew the reason why. But she wasn't sure...

'Ellie, will you please say something?' Patrick demanded at her continued silence.

Was there a time and place to lose that pride she had been trying so desperately to hang on to? And was this the time and place?

'For days now I've had trouble stopping you from saying things I *didn't* want to hear, and now I want you to say something—anything—you've been struck dumb!' he muttered frustratedly. 'Ellie, I'm tired of waiting for you to come to your senses. And I swear, if you don't soon say something I'm going to pick up my father's favourite whisky decanter and throw it out the window!'

Once again Ellie couldn't help it; she laughed. 'And what good will that do?' she finally sobered enough to ask. 'Except break a perfectly beautiful decanter and let in all the frosty air from outside!'

'It's preferable to the overwhelming urge I have right now to wring your beautiful neck!' Patrick rasped.

Tears filled her eyes now. But they were tears of joy, not sadness. 'Patrick—Oh, Patrick—' It was no good. She couldn't talk through the emotion that choked her.

His expression softened slightly before he moved to wrap her fiercely in his arms. 'Ellie, I can't stand this any more! I love you,' he told her forcefully. 'I've loved you for so long, it seems—since the moment I called at your house in the summer, walked round to the garden and saw you lying there—'

'Patrick!' she protested as once again he reminded her of the embarrassment of being caught out bathing topless. Only to become very still in his arms as his words fully penetrated her heightened emotions. 'I— Patrick, did you just say that you love me?' She stared up at him unbelievingly.

He nodded, his mouth twisting into a smile as he looked down at her. 'For all the good it's done me!' He sighed heavily. 'I was always under the impression that falling in love would be a joyful experience—not make me feel as if I had been pole-axed!' he muttered disgustedly. 'Of course it might have helped if the woman I fell in love with felt the same way about me, but as it is—'

'Oh, but she does,' Ellie cut in eagerly, her hands tightly gripping his arms as she gazed up at him, a feeling of such joy welling up inside her she felt as if she might burst. 'I mean—I do,' she corrected awkwardly.

'You do?' Patrick repeated slowly.

She smiled shyly. 'I do,' she confirmed huskily.

He looked at her uncertainly now. 'But the other night, when Davies left so abruptly, you were crying—'

'Because of the way he'd kept belittling me in front of you—making me sound like—! Patrick, I only told you that I still cared about Gareth to try and cover up the fact that I've fallen in love with you,' she added softly.

'And all this time I've been going quietly insane with jealousy!' he groaned. 'Ellie, do you love me enough to walk down the aisle to me with Toby at your side, to stand next to me in front of a vicar, with all our family and friends looking on and wishing us well as we make our vows to each other?' he said slowly.

Was Patrick asking her to marry him? It certainly sounded like it!

'A "meaningless affair",' he muttered disgustedly, before Ellie could answer him. 'As if that's what I ever wanted from you!' He moved back slightly, holding her away from him as he looked down at her. 'I love you, Elizabeth Fairfax. Will you marry me?'

She swallowed the tears, gazing up at him adoringly. 'Oh, yes!' she answered joyfully.

His eyes widened. 'You will…?'

'I will,' she confirmed emotionally.

He closed his eyes briefly, as if he couldn't quite

believe what he had just heard, and then those eyes gleamed silver as he looked at her once again.

'Darling Patrick.' Ellie raised a hand to gently touch the hardness of his cheek, making no effort to hide her love for him now, knowing by the sudden glow of emotion in his eyes how deeply affected he was just by the touch of her hand. 'Why did you never tell me before— show me that you felt this way about me?' she choked.

'Because when I first began to feel this way about you I very quickly learnt from Toby that you were involved with Gareth Davies, and had been for several months.' He scowled at the memory. 'Not the best news I'd ever had in my life. Patience is not exactly one of my virtues,' he admitted self-derisively, 'but I decided, when it came to you, I didn't have much choice in the matter; no one else would do for me once I had seen you.'

Ellie could hardly believe all this; Patrick.had been in love with her for months and she had had no idea!

She frowned. 'But I stopped seeing Gareth two months ago...'

Patrick nodded. 'And I'm sure having me turn up on the doorstep with every intention of sweeping you off your feet would have been exactly what you wanted immediately after that!' he drawled. 'No, I decided I had to leave things for a while, give you a chance to get over—whatever.' He scowled again, just at the thought of her ever having felt anything for Gareth. 'It was all I could do to stop myself getting up and hugging Toby when he came to me three weeks ago and asked if I would mind taking you to the Delacorte dinner!' he revealed happily. 'Mind?' he repeated mockingly. 'I ''minded'' so much I followed Toby home that very evening just for the opportunity of seeing you again!'

Ellie winced as she remembered that evening. 'At which time I said thanks, but no thanks. I'm so sorry, Patrick.' She groaned in remorse. 'I really had no idea.'

No idea that he had loved her for months. No idea that all this time she had been fighting her feelings for him he had already been in love with her.

'It doesn't matter.' He shook his head. 'None of that matters if you really do love me.' He still looked as if he couldn't quite believe it was true.

And no wonder, when she had been pushing him away at every opportunity, to the point where she had even claimed to still have feelings for Gareth!

'Patrick, I thought—' She gave a heavy sigh. 'When I found out about Toby and Teresa that evening we came back from dinner, I thought you had just been taking me out to give them enough of a breathing space to convince Toby into announcing their engagement. You were so—definite about Toby's sense of loyalty, how fond he was of me, how he felt a responsibility—'

'But not to the point of my deceiving you in that way!' he instantly protested. 'Was that the reason you suddenly cooled towards me? Another reason you told me that you were still in love with Davies?' he added hopefully.

'Yes,' she confirmed with a grimace.

'Ellie, by saying those things about Toby I was just letting you know that, when the time came I'd fully approve of Toby as my sister's future husband, listing the qualities he had that made me feel that way. I never—' Patrick broke off, shaking his head. 'Ellie, I only ever went out with you because I'm so deeply in love with you I can't think straight half the time! Do you believe me?' He looked down at her intently.

She gave a tremulous smile. 'As long as you tell me that the children you're going to educate from home will be my children too!'

The tension left him and he gathered her close in his arms. 'They were never going to be anyone else's,' he assured her huskily.

Her arms tightened about his waist as she told him fiercely, 'I love you so much, Patrick.'

'I love you, Ellie.' His words were muffled in the dark thickness of her hair. 'Would you mind very much if we were married as soon as it can be arranged? I really don't think I can wait too much longer to make you completely mine,' he owned longingly.

She didn't want to wait either—wanted to be Patrick's wife as much as he wanted to be her husband.

'I don't mind at all,' she assured him huskily. 'But perhaps we should wait until you no longer have a black eye; at the moment you most resemble a panda bear!' she added teasingly.

'As long as you become *Mrs* Panda Bear, who the hell cares?' he dismissed happily.

Certainly not Ellie!

How different everything was now from her unhappiness when the evening had begun. She loved Patrick. He loved her in return. They were going to be married. To each other.

Toby was right; this was going to be the best Christmas ever.

And it was only the start of what promised to be the best years of her life.

Of their life together.

Patrick and Ellie.

How wonderful that sounded!

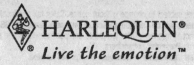

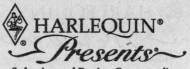

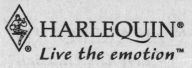

The world's bestselling romance series.

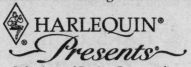

HARLEQUIN®
Presents~

Seduction and Passion Guaranteed!

Legally wed, great together in bed,
but he's never said…"I love you."

They're…

Wedlocked!

The series
in which
marriages are
made in haste…
and love
comes later…

Don't miss

THE TOKEN WIFE by Sara Craven,
#2369 on sale January 2004

Coming soon

THE CONSTANTIN MARRIAGE by Lindsay Armstrong,
#2384 on sale March 2004

**Pick up a Harlequin Presents® novel and you will
enter a world of spine-tingling passion and
provocative, tantalizing romance!**

Available wherever Harlequin books are sold.

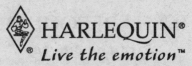

HARLEQUIN®
Live the emotion™

Visit us at www.eHarlequin.com

HPWEDJF

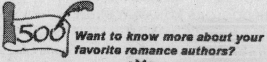

The world's bestselling romance series.

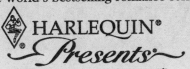

HARLEQUIN® *Presents*

Seduction and Passion Guaranteed!

INTERNATIONAL
DOCTORS

They're guaranteed to raise your pulse!

Meet the most eligible medical men of the world, in a new series of stories, by popular authors, that will make your heart race!

Whether they're saving lives or dealing with desire, our doctors have got bedside manners that send temperatures soaring....

Coming in Harlequin Presents in 2003:

THE DOCTOR'S SECRET CHILD by Catherine Spencer
#2311, on sale March

THE PASSION TREATMENT by Kim Lawrence
#2330, on sale June

THE DOCTOR'S RUNAWAY BRIDE by Sarah Morgan
#2366, on sale December

Pick up a Harlequin Presents® novel and you will enter a world of spine-tingling passion and provocative, tantalizing romance!

Available wherever Harlequin books are sold.

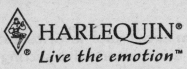

HARLEQUIN®
Live the emotion™

Visit us at www.eHarlequin.com

HPINTDOC